Other works by Andrew Forrest Baker:

Short Stories

Roast, a short story

Longer Stories

Hymn

WE TREMBLE AS WE SINK

Cover and book design by Andrew Forrest Baker.

Published 2011 by Squid & Ego Press.

WE
TREMBLE

AS   WE

SINK

TABLE OF
CONTENTS

OUR HOUSE IS SOUND

MOST DAYS

& ON THE DAYS

IT IS NOT, WE

FIGURE

OUT A MEANS OF

CONTAINMENT

WE
TREMBLE
AS   WE
SINK

RooT
RoT

The crops withered upward, root rot killing first the stem and then the leaves, so rapidly that the brown grew like a shadow across the field. The dismal display extended outward toward the end of the property, jumped the fence and continued on toward the Cypress, or further yet, into the waters.

The pulpating larva of the cromwell beetles feasted from the softened root work of the grass's life support. The corn released from its sheath to reveal blackened kernels, all of them withering, whole pockets of life disintegrating at the touch.

The tomatoes sagged on the vines until their bottoms gave out and the fruit popped forth from the skin. First red, then brown, then quickly ash. The okra had not even been pollinated when they were struck down. The white flowers turned black and drooped before the bees or the wind or the humidity could move the pollen to the pistol. A week later and there could have been a nice harvest of the pods, a week later and there coulda been something to eat with the plant's short leap to harvest.

The bugs all feasting sounded loudly; drones of locusts descending. The beans silenced. The sun set early, ashamed to look on us any longer. The final cries of life struggled from the soil. The land finally gave in.

We have to walk, caterwauling, down the hallways after dusk so that the wolves hidden between the panels of the floorboards are afraid to sneak out and strike. It's a habit left over from before there were even walls, when the wooden planks were the trees, and the glowing eyes nursed the canine brains toward the hunt. It's a habit left over from before we were born.

Our house is sound, most days, so it's really only in the hallways where we have to keep on our toes. Once, maybe two or three winters back, the storm window came lose in one of the second story bedrooms, and Pa liked to have a stroke trying to figure out where that rattling sound was coming from every time the wind blew north-easternly. It took us nearly two weeks to figure out it was that thick piece of glass, polished clean, banging back and forth between the screen and the rose-colored trellis frame that enclosed the actual window. But that's a rarity. Our house is sound, most days, and on the days it is not, we figure out a means of containment.

It's the nights we have to worry about.

Sometimes, when we're all sitting in the house, when all the work is done, we let our hands trace along the hardwood floors. We sit there, Indian-style, our bare feet warmed beneath the denim, and watch our fingers seek out the knots in the boards. They're oak, the boards, most of them, but some of them are from the cypress trees that used to tower out back. We shoved them in ourselves, wherever they'd fit

best, so that, really, it's only us who can understand the pattern they make. A few though already need to be replaced; the softwood sags beneath our steps.

The sun lights the dark spots on the planks, and we let our fingers swish gingerly across where Mama's smile would have been.

Most folks, they think there ain't no more wolves in the swamp, but we know better. Most people will say the wolves all got hunted out, or else they figured out that the bog isn't all that hospitable and hightailed it on out. They ignore the howls at night, pretend they didn't hear nothing, or maybe they blame the noises on the South Georgia Pig Man out searching the grounds for some deer to gut or fisherman to scare, but we know the truth. We know there's still wolves and that they reckoned on a way to live with the tepid waters, that they figured out a way of living forever.

When Pa died, that's when we stopped going into town. We didn't like the idea of being state property any more than we liked having to use our last two fifty-cent pieces to keep him blind and pay his way up to Heaven. But we figured we couldn't spend it none at the market anyway without drawing attention to ourselves, and that, anyway, penny candy was out of the question.

On occasion, a hen would get out over at Ms. Maybelle's—who lived a ways down across the water—and end up in our yard. We'd eat pretty well for a coupla days and then a sow would turn up and we could feast for weeks. We were of a mind to think sometimes that it was Ol' Maybelle herself who was chasing the livestock to- wards us, but whenever we'd catch sight of her across the bog she never once smiled or waved.

The outside world is much brighter at night than most people give it credit for. From inside the house we watch the night air alight with fireflies in their incandescent call-and-response mating dance. Some nights we get the will-o'-the-wisp and the burning off of decay slipping into the air, like the life part of it was finally released and the world has to temporarily explode to absorb it back in. Some nights we get the swamp gas, and only we can spot the difference between what is what, and then it's every night we get the red eyes of the wolves.

In the moments just when night sets in, when the air is still warm and hazy from the sunshine that was searing down, that's when we feel them start to stir. The wind that's coming off the bog twists and jetties to avoid the gnats, to trickle a few leaves here, a few blades of grass there, and maybe the fur around their jaws. The cicadas emerge from their brown shells, leave 'em clinging to tree trunks and wisteria vines, and twitch their hind legs together with all their might, the roosters of dusk calling all the night creatures to arms. When they're especially loud, when the whimpers beneath the house start to vibrate the wood nails and the old iron pots Mama left hanging in the kitchen, that's when we pull out her old gramophone.

Mama, she loved the opera. She'd made her way over to Mobile once, before we was born, and Pa liked to joke that those big city lights had never left her eye. She'd laugh her woodpecker laugh and say with a flourish of her skirt that the light in her eye was just Pa and us, and then put on one of those records with the warbling arias and try to sing along to the falsettos.

When the cicadas and the wolves get particularly loud, we put on those records too. We aim the horn of the gramophone out the window, out over the peat grass and pretty soon the whole swamp, all the nocturnal parts of it, everything is all swaying along at a syncopated pace.

If we know the rhythm, sometimes the wolves are easier to evade.

On nights that we're especially afraid of the hallways, we sit in the living room with Mama and Pa. It's always pitch black, and we push the mat aside to sit with our backs to the front door, letting our eyes adjust so we can make out two of the cypress patterns in the floorboards. The June bugs click against the screen door and we let our ears map out the jumble of their movements at our backs. Mama used to hate June bugs. She would scream as they'd bang against the windowpanes and crawl a crisscross on the porch light when we'd sit taking our evening tea or lemonade in the springtime dusk. Or if she were hanging out the laundry and one of their little brown beetle bodies clung tight onto the sheets, she holler so as you might think the Pig'an'd done made it out of the bog and was set upon her. Pa'd take off to running fast around the house and swat the bug away and Mama'd call him her hero and they'd laugh about it while we watched from the water's edge and the toy boat armada we'd made of folded paper got consumed by the swishing and sank down. We knew if we waited long enough those paper boats would make their way back up, but they wouldn't be usable anyway so we'd turn our backs on the water and skip up toward Mama and Pa and ask what we were having for dinner.

Everything that sinks down in the swamp has a way of rising back up again. That's how come we knew the floorboards were a safer bet than the marsh waters. We were eleven when we lost Mama, and we already understood that about the mire. We were eleven when we lost Mama and twelve when we lost Pa, but in all fairness it was in the span of one night. Mama went before the midnight of our birthday and Pa was gone soon after. We had to wish ourselves a happy twelve years of living and the two dollars our parents had left for us on the kitchen table beside the card and the balloon to surprise us at breakfast, the four fifty-cent pieces went right back to them to buy their ways off this plane. Two to Mama just before midnight; our last two to Pa just after. They went right back to them to keep them blind.

We didn't go to school the next day because it took us a while to get the oak flooring to move. Eventually we figured we'd just have to smash up the boards. And we couldn't go to school the day after that 'cause we needed to down one of the Cypress in the back to cover Mama and Pa so they'd be at peace. And after that there was work to be done around the house, laundry and pruning, and hemming and hawing and scratching and spitting—all those things our parents had once done—and so our days became pretty much occupied.

When Mister Clarence showed up at our doorstep one day, we weren't at all surprised. He was the county truancy officer and he'd be obligated to come and check out where 'bouts we'd gotten to. We sat with our backs up against the front door like a barricade, our fingers tracing the knots in the floorboards while we waited to hear his footsteps departing. What did surprise us though was the sound a few minutes later of the screen door slamming on the kitchen side of the house and Mister Clarence's footsteps making their way into the living room where we were waiting. In that moment, in the heat of it all and the heat of the July shade, there weren't many options we had, really. And Mama and Pa had the coins so they didn't see a thing.

Mister Clarence had had to park his car about a mile back—it's amazing how fast a driveway can grow over in the summer heat and damp of the bog—so it was nearly a month or so before anyone made their way over to our place to check up on him. It was another state official, but a petty one, not like a sheriff or a deputy or anything, and we never learned his name before he went to join Mister

Clarence.

We cut down another Cypress.

The swamp muddles. The blackwaters remain all tied up with the peat moss, even as currents push out toward the Gulf of Mexico to the south, push east down the St. Marys to the Atlantic. The waters in our backyard, they just stop. On the surface they rest all sedentary 'cept for when a gator peaks out. On the surface they sleep all soundly in the moss and the ferns and the cypress roots and the mud. And we have to walk above the surface. We have to learn to step gingerly so the stillness doesn't get a chance to catch us.

It's easier to wrangle this barefoot, which is good for us since our toes outdone our shoes about a month or so back and Pa's old soles just hang and fidget on our feet. Without them though, we can almost waltz out the right sequence of steps through the house without even thinking about it. We know which steps we have to twist our big toe up over the next two before the light down. We know when to make our knees jump backwards and how to make our arms follow suit so as we can keep our balance. We almost never hit the Cypress anymore so we rarely get the mist of the wolves breath on our heels.

It's been about six months since anyone else made his or her way out here. We figure local legend took hold and since no one but Ms. Maybelle knows we're here anyway, no one was brave enough to come out looking. People go missing all the time in the swamp as it is. And after seven folks done evaporated in near 'bouts the same place—more if our family is included—the townsfolk just chalk it up to a bog witch or a panther or the Pig'an or the motorboats of the drug cartel passing through. So the townsfolk really just figured it better off to leave the place alone.

It was better off for us too, seeing as how our hallway was almost wholly cypress now and getting harder and harder to navigate. The howling helps, especially at night, and we dug through every drawer in Pa's room looking for more half-dollars to try to blind out a few of the wolves beneath the floorboards, but we never did find any. So we yell as we move down the hallway, hopscotching on the few oak boards left, until we reach our rooms and can finally get some rest.

He said it sounded like a she-'possum's screech when one of her young'uns done dropped from her pouch, somersaulting down from that pine branch perch and ker plunking to the undergrowth below. The scream. That blood-curdling shriek. And of course he went running, 'cause that's just how he was. A good man. An honest man. No matter how crazy you could say—and rightfully so—Holton Martin was, you could not deny his downright kindness.

Most times that scream was emanating from the pretty little lungs of some weekend warrior socialite, down from the big city in her off-road SUV for a weekend of "roughing it" in the secured campgrounds of the National Park. She and her husband and their cockadoodle or puggle or whatever other canine they felt it necessary to cross with the toy dog du jour would be out trying to prove to Greenpeace and the EPA that they really were true environmentalists. She and her beau, they'd have just set up their tent and sleeping bags and strapped up their solar-powered outdoor shower to some low-hanging branch, and he'd have gone off to gather up some wood to start a fire with the kerosene and store-bought kindling they'd brought in from the city, and she'd swear she saw a giant gator or some ferocious black bear bearing down on her with glistening white fangs. She'd let out that scream, and old Holt would set to running.

"Only once I done seen an actual bear get-

tin' into their food stash, munching on those raw wieners and gettin' his gums all sticky on the marshmallows," Holt told us, swigging on his 'shine, pounding on the clapboard bar at Grayson's Spirits and Eats to punctuate his story.

Grayson's was the place all the local men flocked to when the gnats got so thick outside they looked like Spanish moss dancing through the cypress groves, billowing black and gray and lumines-cent from the South Georgia humidity. Neal Grayson's pappy, Ar-nold, had started the place way back when, and Neal still kept that brass-tacks still pumping away in the basement. 'Bout ten-years back, Duke Bellows, the local sheriff and a man whose laugh lived up to his name, made a half-hearted attempt to shut the bar down in order to appease the voters living on the cul de sacs in the subdivid-ed parts of the county, but in all honesty, he loved that rotgut drip-ping out of the basement just as much as the rest of us. Duke'd even donated one of the seven stuffed gator heads decorating the walls around the raw-plank shelves and the torn-label liquor bottles as an apology for the media-affront he'd caused the place. Neal didn't care none though: said it brought in a whole new cast of tourist-customers willing to pay top dollar for some authentic backwoods sour mash.

"This lady today though," Holt said, stifling his guffaw with an immediate intensity to his grin, "she was damn set sure she'd seen the Pig'an. I thought I smelt him too when I got there, but way I fig-ure, I reckon ol' Colt done got there 'fore I did and scared 'im off."

That was the disordered part of Holton Martin's brain, the crazy part. Not his unwavering belief in the South Georgia Pig Man–that Bigfoot of the swamp with sightings dating back a couple hundred years and probably continuing for a couple hundred years more–but his unmitigated assurance that his twin brother was out there in the peat moss bog. Colton had died nearly fifty-seven years ago, a couple of hours after birth. His parents had named him Colt because, as they'd told Holt, that little boy had wanted to run free like the horses. But Holt had spent the past fifty-seven years or so whispering secrets out into the waterways, buying two sets of all his clothing to leave one on the porch for Colt to pick up. The fact that they always disappeared just reassured Holt that Colt was out there. And seeing as I'm about the same size and build as the old man, I got a few new shirts a year if I could get there before the 'coons, and if not, they got some nice plaid accents to their nests.

"I tell you what, though, fellas," Holt's voice hummed above the rising din as more men and a woman or two circled in closer to hear or order another drink or try their luck at a smile before the moonshine could kick in, "that whole campsite reeked of the Pig'an. You know, that scent like someone done took a shit in a deer carcass and left it out to ripe on the side of the road. I bet those yup-pies hopped right back in their Range Rover and ranged their rove right back up to Atlanta. Hell, I wouldn'ta even slept there with the Pig'an's smell hovering around like that."

The Pig'an, as most of the folks whose slow dialect couldn't afford the time for the "m" referred to our local Sasquatch, was one of our most popular local legends. Everybody's grandpa's hunting buddy had seen him, and all the front porch stories put the brute at just under seven feet with a furry body, accentuated thumbs, and an upturned nose on his pink-skinned face. Talk was there'd been a whole family of them at one point, roaming through the swamp, feasting on a dead deer or perhaps a wounded owl, and mostly keep-ing to the shadows. Others asserted that there'd only ever been one, that he was descended from the native tribes who'd once danced their rain dances and built their burial mounds here, that he'd been born a freak and his tribe had forced him out, and he still roamed the swamps in a sad solitude. However he came to be, the locals all agreed that he was best viewed after a swift chug of Albert's finest and then only out of the corner of the eye. The alcohol took the edge off the scent, they'd say, and opened up your mind to the possibili-ties of seeing. And then most everybody'd laugh at the thrill chasers who'd get all wide-eyed and mentally overactive as they headed out to set up their tents. I'd never once seen the Pig'an, not even in pass-ing, but, even if they'd laugh at the campers, most folks around here still believed in his possibility.

"Well, boys," I said into the general din of conversations cater-wauling about the bar, "I best to be getting off home."

I got a few nods in acknowledgement as I tossed a couple bills to Neal and made my way out into the late evening humidity. I could feel Holt's eyes following me all the way to the door. Behind me, the men continued their talking as if, for all intents and purposes, I'd never even been there, which, I thought sometimes, they'd just as reckon I never was.

I'd come to the swamp about ten years prior from down in Tallahassee, Florida after I couldn't shake the feeling that the peat bogs were where I needed to be. Emancipated from my parents at fifteen after finding out I was adopted at twelve, I'd spent a few years wandering around the coastal cities along the Gulf of Mexico, hocking tie-dyed tee-shirts in the Red Neck Riviera or Mai Tai's in Fort Myers before buckling down and heading up to Tallahassee to learn veterinary medicine. When I graduated I heard tell of a position treating animals in the National Park and settled down in this Podunk town in the deep south of the Georgia south. That was two strikes against me though, as far as the locals were concerned: working for the government and being from Florida. 'Cause as far as the natives figured, anybody from Florida was really just a migrant northerner and anybody working for the federal government was really just an intruder on their way of life. But I got the dialect down real quick-like, and turned my practice from working directly for the park into an independent business, helping the local community pets and the sick creatures from the bogs, even housing the latter who, once they got well enough, were shipped around from elementary school to elementary school to teach the kids about the critters of the mire. And I'd helped out a few of the men there hanging around Grayson's enough times that I was less of an outsider than some, but still not completely in the fold.

Without getting inside, I reached into my pickup and cranked her up, letting the engine warm up and the AC cool down a bit before I started my ride home. The sun was setting through the trees to the west, casting an eerie glow on the haze that perpetually circumnavigated the swamp, always off there in the distance, but rarely where you could catch up to it. I pulled myself up to the hood of my truck and lit up a cigarette, letting my eyes follow the mating dance of the lightning bugs beginning to flicker back and forth, wondering if the burning cherry on my smoke confused the ritual at all. It was moments like these, sweltering in the heat, watching the fireflies dance, hearing the growing song of the cicadas melt with the murmuring yammer from the folks in the bar, that made me glad I'd ended up here.

Across the lot, Charles hopped out from the bed of Duke's truck and plodded his way over to my feet. I slipped down from my hood and stroked the hound between his ears as he sniffed around my palms and pockets for a biscuit. It was more of a reflex than anything else, his sniffing. His nose had stopped working a good two years back. But old habits die pretty hard, I reckon.

"I'm sorry, buddy," I said, as frankly as I could, "I don't have any treats on me this time."

Charles huffed into my face, but sat down by my side anyway, allowing me to stroke under his chin. I'd never been one to baby talk to an animal, and I thought they responded better to the upfront demeanor in my voice. Charles had been a member of the force for a good six or seven years before his sniffer'd gone kaput. They'd used him mostly to help search out folks who'd gone hiking off the trails and lost their way. Once or twice he'd been used on a drug bust, but that was rare 'round these parts. Not the drugs so much as the busts, I guess. After his nose had gone out, Duke had taken him in, but old Charles was still very much a dog about town.

I gave his belly a good strong pat as I began to stand up. His ears perked as I rose, well before I heard the Trans Am barreling down the gravel road behind me, a good twenty or thirty miles above the speed limit. We both watched the car fly by, churning up a cloud of dust and exhaust in its wake.

"Tourists," I said to Charles, knowing he'd take me as a native any day, and he whimpered in response. I leaned down to give him one last rub, but he let out a wail and set off running after the Trans Am.

That's when I heard the crash.

It wasn't all loud and clangy and metallic like they make them sound in the movies, but more of a dim thud, a little splash of water. Some grinding. I called into Grayson's after Duke and ran after Charles, leaving my truck there idling in the parking lot. Charles was waiting for me around the bend, and, when he saw I was following, started running once more toward the wreck.

Best I could tell, the car had crossed over the lanes and hopped to the ditch head on. The front end was raised a bit, wrapped around a pine, the wheels still spinning at top speed. The back wheels were sinking into the mud, and the Florida license plate was splattered with red clay and pollen. Charles was whooping and hollering, darting back and forth behind the car, leaping up toward the driver's side window. As I drew closer, the engine died and the wheels slowed to a halt. Behind me, I heard Duke and Holt running forward, spitting out profanities as they came.

I reached to clasp the door handle and get to the driver, when Duke yelled out to stop me.

"Don't fuck up my crime scene!" he slurred, trying to shake off the whiskey and shake in his professional demeanor.

"It's a wreck, not a crime scene," I called back. "The driver may need a doctor!"

"You ain't no people doctor," Duke snapped back, reaching my side and going for the door, "so lessen the driver's a porcupine I can take it from here."

I stood back from the vehicle, joining Holt back on the road as he did his best to keep the onlookers pouring out of Grayson's from pushing their way up to the Trans Am's windows.

"Besides," Duke mumbled from behind us as he leaned into the smoking vehicle, "ain't no kind of doctor gonna do this guy no good."

There were about seven or eight men now, grouping up in the street, trying to peek through the tinted back window of the car, mumbling to themselves about the tourists and the local kids and their reckless driving. One of them got off on how "reckless" seemed like such an inappropriate word considering the current circumstances, and a few of the other men began to laugh and push forward on Holt and me. I spotted Neal coming up and broke away from Holt to beg him to do what he could to get the men away from the scene and back into the bar. I'd fixed up his wife's cat for free when she'd gotten clawed once by an owl, so he figured he owed me.

"Come on, boys," Neal called out. "Next round's on me. I still got a couple bottles left from when my pop runned the still."

Alert to the notion of Arnold's old stash, the men lost their rubbernecking tendencies for the rotgut rumble. I nodded to Neal as he glanced toward me, silently letting me know that his "on me" had really meant on me, and he turned to herd the men back toward his place. Duke joined Holt and me by the side of the road.

"Keep this area secured," he insisted. "I need to get back to my truck and call this in."

Holt and I stood in silence as the men rounded the bend and made their way back through Grayson's parking lot. Behind us, the steam whistling out from under the Trans Am's banged up hood began to whine in a lower pitch before sputtering to a stop. The silence that had immediately followed the crash was lost to the rising sound of the insects welcoming the night stars, and Holt handed me the flashlight he'd had strapped to a buckle on the waist of his overalls.

"You reckon Duke's really calling this in or trying to nab hisself a jar of Arnold's lightning?" Holt asked me, smiling and nodding his head toward the still open car door. "That poor bastard may not need a doctor, but maybe getting some doctor's eyes on 'im'd be good for appeasin' the fam'ly some."

The driver couldn't have been more than twenty years old. His scraggly brown hair looked like it hadn't been washed in weeks and covered half his face as his body leaned forward, suspended by his safety belt between the seatback and the steering column. The bruising from where his forehead had struck against the wheel was peaking out from under the oily locks. The veins in his arms glowed a fierce blue next to his sallow skin in the beam from my flashlight. His lips, too, seemed awfully washed out for someone who'd died not twenty minutes before.

I let the beam of my flashlight dance through the cab of the car. Nothing. The car was remarkably clean for someone as unkempt as the recently deceased boy in the driver's seat. As my gaze reached the floorboard, I noticed a stick lodged against the gas pedal, holding it to the floor even after the engine'd done given up hope and petered out.

"I don't think this was an accident," I told Holt as we listened to the siren from Duke's deputy vehicles approaching from the east. "That kid in there; he's been dead at least a day 'fore now."

"Well, I'll be damned," Holt said, taking his flashlight from me and flagging Deputy Squalls down to scene. "I reckon it's done near 'bout time for the swamp to start its rising up again."

Nearly two weeks went by before we saw the first van, its glistening lily white veneer growing dusty and red as it rambled down the back roads searching for a place to set up shop near the scene of the accident. Before long there were two more, each of them sporting a different tri-colored logo on their sliding doors just below the moss gray satellite dishes mounted to their roofs, all angling up and away from the pines to suss out the best signal. Tallahassee, Albany, and Valdosta had all taken note and we knew it wouldn't be long until Atlanta and Mobile made their way down.

Duke'd done pretty well at keeping the details of the crash under wraps, but as soon as the body was ID'd as the party-boy son of some Nashville Rising Star, the news crews started rolling in. We figured we had another day or so before the town was packed with vans and paparazzi, all angling for the scoop; for the best shot of the bumper marks the Trans Am left on the evergreen.

We'd only managed to last this long without the news crews because the body had taken so long to tell us who he was. His wallet had no ID or credit cards, just twenty-seven cents and a receipt from a gas station over in Bainbridge. The car, it turned out, was a rental, last picked up in Tampa, and the guy whose name it was out under was sleeping soundly in his bed when the uniforms in Miami went by with a photo to get the body ID'd and break the bad news to his wife. He'd never seen the kid, nor did he remember renting any car. Dental records finally gave the kid away as Burt Tracy from Nashville, and suddenly all the news beat hotlines lit up with the notion of getting the big scoop. Burt's father was wrapping up a tour in Texas when he got told, and he hadn't made it down to the coroner's office yet to claim the body, but we figured once he had, the vans would start to vanish.

"Arch confirmed your note about the time of death," Duke whispered to me as we crossed the gravel lot at Grayson's toward my pickup, doing our best to avoid the microphones in the hands of bored looking reporters sitting on the floorboards of their open minivans, waiting for word of any new development or to smile their "live from Folkston" during the eight o'clock airing. "He said cause of death looked like blunt trauma to the back of the head which wasn't consistent with the crash, and also that the kid had high levels of MDMA in his system. So at least we know he died happy."

Duke smiled at me, and I tried to keep my furrowed brow from betraying my confusion at him letting me in on his confidential information. Duke didn't outright dislike me, but he'd never been close to extending a welcoming arm for me to enter his Big Boy's circle. All I could guess was that, since he knew I'd looked at the body, I already had it figured out. Plus he'd been impressed by my sighting of the lodged gas pedal. I'd followed him back east along the road on the night of the crash, out to the nearest bend, the only spot the Trans Am could have started from in accordance to where it went over, but the rushing sedans of the deputies arriving on the scene had stripped the dirt road of any tire treads from whatever vehicles carried away the folks who'd tried to stage the accident. He hadn't said anything to me then, just mumbled something about me not quite getting the difference between men and road kill, but tonight he was all smiles and information.

"Best I can make it," the old sheriff went on, "the kid OD'd at one of those crazy rave dance parties the kids in Florida like to have, fell and banged his noggin on the floor of whatever warehouse they were illegally using, and some of his dopey friends decided to make it look like an accident so as they wouldn't get into trouble. There weren't no other prints on the car or on that stick, so we just decided it'd be best to keep it out of the news so the reporters can take off and things can get back to normal around here."

The last part he said with a direct glare into my eyes. That was why he was confiding in me, to make sure I was keeping my mouth shut too. If there was anything our local law enforcement offices were known for, it was quick solutions and a rapid mainte-nance of the traditional way of life. They kept the occasional drunk-and-disorderly wandering the sidewalks beside the Masonic Hall or the Baptist Church easily under wraps. They ensured the Florida couples taking advantage of us being the Marriage Capital of the South (our colloquially term since Vegas had taken over the "World" title) got their fix of our no-wait marriage period at the courthouse and clanged their tin-can-car-trains right back down the highway without too much ado. They were quite adept at keeping the more surreptitious aspects of our little backwoods society quiet. And, ap-parently, Duke figured he could keep me quiet as well.

"Thanks for letting me stay abreast, Sheriff." Duke took my hand as I reached for the armrest and pulled myself up into the truck. "You give my regards to Charles."

As I slammed the door shut, he rested his thick, calloused hands on the ledge of the open driver's side window.

"You get what I'm saying to you, right, son?"

His face was red and sullen, and I took a moment while light-ing my cigarette to really take in his features. The deep, necrotic lines that circled his thin, pale lips revealed the rapid weight loss Duke experienced soon after his glory days of high school football. Each crevice of his jowls was amass with burst capillaries that never seemed to heal, twisting his face into an alternating visage of prima-ry colors; of red, yellow, and blue splotches that hardened his deep brown eyes to a steel-enforced gaze. The hasty retreat of follicles atop his head resulted in pale pink sun exposure barely revealed beneath his brown derby-styled hat. Everything about Duke Bel-lows screamed sudden, as if his body was reacting to his personal-ity. Or maybe his personality was reacting to his genetic structure. The veins stretched taut across his knuckles throbbed in a slightly syncopated pulse as his grip tightened against the red aluminum of my truck.

"I have no reason to talk to any newshounds," I assured him, allowing the seconds for the customary nod before I pulled the gear shaft into reverse.

Sue yawned a lazy greeting in my direction as I got out of the pickup before she returned to snapping her massive jaws around the dandelion blooms that littered my yard. She deftly severed the stems, allowing those that had not yet gone to seed to rest atop her tongue, mandible and maxilla slightly ajar with a brilliant yellow gleam. Watching her there reminded me of my youth, of my mother showing me the golden glow the flowers could project upon our chins, of her telling me the opaqueness of the reflection meant one person liked butter more so than the other. My skin, darker than hers, barely revealed the mustard that shone from her chin. I saw her chin, her cheeks, her eyes turn red as my father yelled at me, as he told me I was never really his son and I never really could be.

Every now and then the swift flash of a firefly would catch Sue's attention, and we'd both turn to watch it echo through the marsh as potential mates answered the call. I reached down to loosen the rope around her neck and rubbed the skin along her fore-left shoulder, giving my best attempt at comforting the phantom limb pain that had, most likely, long since resided. Sue barely took any notice of the rope, loosened or tightened, around her neck, aware as she was that the twine itself was no match for the power within her body. She waited for me beside the pile of wood I kept chopped for the nights that bonfires seemed appropriate as I made my way up to the mailbox I'd posted up at the end after the letter carriers had rallied up and refused to drop off my post in the box up on the porch on account of the three-legged alligator roaming around the property. I liked the way the ax-blade looked there, nestled within a half-split log like the pictures in the Cub Scout books my adoptive parents had made me study to earn the little round embroidered merit badges. It made me feel rustic, manly.

When I started my trek back toward the house, Sue seemed satisfied that I was in for the evening and gave up her post to swish her tail in the small koi pond I'd dug out for her. It wasn't very big, just barely enough for her to submerge her body if she curled in her tail, but it was predator-free and easy for her to pull herself out of, even with only the strength of one fore-appendage.

I double-checked the lock on the front door of the house to make sure Marty had left it secure and headed around back to where I'd converted things into my own living quarters. Marty was a bright kid, and I paid him to come 'round twice a week to feed the critters boarded in the vet side of the building, but once or twice he'd left the door unlocked or wide open and trotted off home only to deny it when I confronted him about it. But overall he was a good kid, and he didn't get disgusted at feeding the snakes or cleaning out the cages. Plus I liked having a couple nights a week where I could make off into town and not worry about the goings-on back at work.

The back door was ajar when I made it around, looking violent in its incorrect placement amidst the rest of the rear of my house. I pulled myself inside and followed the path to the door dividing home and office, also swung open, walking as quietly as possible and trying to listen for any noise beyond the pounding pulse in my ear. There was faint breathing coming from one of the operating rooms. I grabbed hold of a scalpel from the autoclave room, quietly removing the antiseptic packaging and holding the blade out as a weapon. Hoping whoever was in there didn't come with a shotgun, I pushed open the door to the OR and jabbed my 36 blade blindly before me. Hitting nothing, I peered around the room. Cabinets were open, but the contents of each of them seemed intact. Then I saw Marty. His body hidden by the island table, the red hair poking from behind it was unmistakably his. His forehead was paler than usual. I dropped the blade and moved forward. His pulse was strong despite his shallow breathing.

I called the cops and his dad, then propped up his head and tried at waking him up in case whatever had knocked him out had also given him a concussion. His eyes fluttered a bit, opening for the most part, but his gaze remained vacant even as the sirens grew louder outside. The ambulance backed its way up to my porch as Duke stepped from his patrol car.

"Don't touch anything in there 'til I get a look around," he called to the paramedics. Then to me: "The boy's fine, right? Not dead or dying or anything. He can hold tight for a minute more."

I nodded to Duke with a cocked eyebrow and led the crew that had just arrived back to where Marty was lying, still on the floor, but with his head propped up under one of my sweatshirts. The paramedics stood off to one side after checking the kid's pulse and making sure his pupils were dilating and Duke stepped around the room with his eyes darting over everything. He asked the usual barrage of questions—where were you... anything missing... any idea who—and let his foot roll over the scalpel I'd dropped to the floor. He nodded for the paramedics to collect Marty.

"You ain't got no gun, boy?" Duke asked me as the men began to load Marty onto the cart. "You know this little blade here ain't gonna be no good against most of the men 'round these parts. Boys here are born with pistols. Boys who are born here are."

Marty's dad, Rick, stormed into the room and looked relieved when he saw his boy alive if not quite alert. His face relaxed as if a dam had broken, sagging around the corners of his mouth and at the eyelids. His eyes jumped from Marty to survey the room, touching briefly on every cabinet door before landing on Duke and me.

"Robbery gone wrong," Rick said, like it should have been obvious to all of us. "Anything missing?"

"He says there ain't. He didn't notice anything," Duke answered for me.

"Marty must've scared 'em off, before they got to anything." Rick's voice was calm and collected. He spoke carefully, without betraying any worry for the teenage son the paramedics were wheeling from the room. "He's a good kid to have around."

"We'll see," Duke answered. "You want to ride with him up to County? Have him checked out there?"

Rick nodded and left the room. Duke rolled the scalpel over with his boot once more. He stooped to pick it up and laid it on the counter next to the operating table. He reached up and pushed a cabinet door closed.

"If you notice anything missing, give me a ring. Though I think it's probably fine. Probably just some of Marty's buddies from school rough housing and things got out of hand. Just the same, you let me know if you notice anybody hanging around."

After Duke left, I checked after the few dogs that were boarded in the kennel while their owners were vacationing in Panama City and secured the doors to my place, leaving the tiny bit of a mess left over from whatever had happened to clean up in the morning, and grabbed a beer from my fridge. From my back porch, I had a nice view of the waterway, and the government issued airboat I'd gotten when I signed on to doctor up the critters that got hurt on the State Park property was rocking along the side of the mini dock that only rushed out about three feet from the shore. Sue came around the building and pulled herself along beside me as I made my way down to the water, but turned away with about ten feet left to go and returned to her koi pond. She hadn't gotten over losing her arm out there in the swamp, which only endeared her to me all the more.

The sun had taken its time setting, slowed down by the thickness of the air, turning the moisture of the atmosphere brilliant pinks and oranges for what seemed hours before giving up to the darkness. I listened to the night set in, my feet planted on the bed of the boat and legs bending with the bobbing of her hull in the water. Another airboat, its propeller loud and distant hummed through the waterways, obscured by the trees and the Spanish Moss and the density of a nature trying to regain some sense of control. That's when I saw it, resting on the bench of the boat, a fist-sized hunk of granite holding it in place. I knocked the rock aside, picking up the photograph to study in the dimmed rays of light reaching down from my back porch. It was Marty, looking more like his dad in the picture than I'd ever noticed before, wisps of his bright red hair peeking out from beneath a black hoodie, shaking hands with someone who looked like that kid. The one from the Trans Am. The country singer's kid. I flipped the photo over expecting to find some clarification. It was blank. There was nothing else new on my boat, just the rock and the picture. It didn't seem so much like a warning as it did an explanation, but even in that it was obscure. I shoved it into my jacket pocket and headed back inside.

There was a message on my machine from Rick, letting me know Marty was alright, that he'd come to in the ambulance and couldn't remember what had happened, thought maybe he'd slipped on some cat piss or something and knocked his head. None of which made much sense, but it was clear that both Rick and Marty wanted to put the event in the past and just move on from it. A southern man's pride is a tricky thing to maneuver around.

"Just the same," Rick's delayed, mechanized voice was telling me, "if anything there does come up missing, just let me know and I'll pay you for it straight out. No need on getting Duke involved. Or the insurance companies. I can just take care of it myself. And Marty says he's sorry as all get out."

By eight the next morning, I had a line of people pooled up on my front porch, their pets or their neighbor's pets yipping at each other's heels. Whether or not Rick Jacobs wanted word spreading around town about what had happened to his son, the ambulance barreling down the street the previous evening had alerted all the looky-lous out trying for the tidbits. I didn't have a single appointment scheduled, and the money made off a run-of-the-mill checkup was worth the tedium of the townsfolk trying to snoop out some gossip, even if the majority of my day would be spent repeating the same "it weren't no big deal"s in my best colloquial tongue. I was just about to open up the front door to start seeing people in when Duke pounded his fists across the window and motioned for me to let him have a word. I motioned him around back and let him in as quietly as I could manage so as not to start the rumor mill churning up front.

"You got quite the flock of geese gathered on your front stoop there, son," Duke said, waving away the canister of cream I was offering out for the mug of coffee I'd poured him. "Listen up: something just ain't sitting right with me about Rick and Marty's story. Did you clean up any cat piss last night before I got here? I mean, 'tweren't any cats even in that room. And all those doors flung open and nothing missing? Did you notice anything else off this morning? Or last night after we left?"

I thought better of telling Duke about the photograph someone had left on my boat. Instead I just sipped on my own mug of coffee and repeated everything I'd told him yesterday. I played Rick's message still blinking away on my answering machine, and Duke just nodded and hummed a bit into his upper lip.

"It just sounds like a concerned, somewhat shaken father, if you ask me," I said when the message finished its cadence. "He just doesn't want a bigger deal made out of this than has to be."

"Yeah, well, all the same. I'd like to send some boys down to search out that room of yours. Now I'm not saying you can't run your business and whatnot. I wouldn't do that to you with all those paying folks in need of your animal expertise. But I would hate to have to charge you with obscuring an investigation or tampering with evidence on account of those nosy hounds sniffing around this place."

"Is this an official investigation?"

"Son, you've been first-on-scene at two different bodies in the past month. All I'm saying is you should mind yours and do your best at preventing the gossip circles from catching wind and trying you before any of us even knows what the hell is happening here. You been here long enough to know how that works, but not so long as to pick yourself up any loyalty when it comes to that jury of your peers."

"And the jury that's assembled on my front porch?"

"I'll take care of them," the sheriff commanded. "You just go ahead and take the day off, go for a ride out on that dingy you got, and try not to uncover any more dead or unconscious folks inside the county limits." Duke placed his cup down on the counter and made his way back toward the door. "Maybe learn how to make a decent cup of joe while you're at it, son."

I couldn't shake the feeling that someone was watching me. I'd let the engine go cold on my boat once I got far enough into the inner workings of the swamp, and was staring at the herons trying their beaks at fishing in the grizzly heat of the afternoon. I hadn't seen a soul in hours, but still could feel eyes peering down on me from somewhere in the underbrush of the little island off to my right. Fierce and unblinking, like a wild dog staring me down, waiting for me to close me eyes, even for a moment, to strike. I'd left a note on my office door, after Duke had cleared away the masses, that had my cell phone number on it in case there was an animal emergency, but I figured Duke had probably placed one of his deputies up the road a bit from my place to either keep tabs on my pickup or prevent any backwoods detectives from making their way up to my place. Maybe it was another one of Duke's goons sent out to make sure I wasn't stirring up any more trouble for him to clean up and keep out of the Daily News. Duke, I was learning, was quite adept at keeping the town ignorant of most of what went on in its recesses. Made me wonder what all had gone on that wasn't bandied about in backyard clothesline canards.

I let the boat drift closer to the island mass and tethered her to the nearest tree I could securely get the rope around, walked a bit inland and sighed up at the haze of green stretched out before me. I was just about to mount the path toward the old Creek Indian burial mound when she stepped out into it, about ten feet in front of me, and stared me down with a chilling recognition.

She was short, or appeared that way at least, hunched a bit in the back and cupping her hands together at her pelvis. Her clothes were hodgepodged together from strips of what must have been fine garments before her scissors got to them, all in muted tones that camouflaged her against the browns and various greens of the bogs. Her wiry hair was swept up atop her head and her eyes burned in my direction, purple they seemed, as if on fire. I hesitated. She didn't look like a threat, but I'd heard stories of the witch women who lived deep inside the mire, gutting deer for their innards and robbing vacationers of their pups and infants.

"It took you long enough to get here," she said. Her voice was strong and unwavering. It didn't crack and cackle like I'd expected it to. "Well, let's get a move on 'fore Duke and his cronies start showing up."

She turned up the path and started taking sure steps away from the water. I felt compelled to follow after her, like she had somehow placed a lead around my neck. I walked quickly in an attempt to catch up, or almost catch up. I wanted to stay a few paces behind her in order to keep her in my sight.

She didn't speak as we walked, seeming instead to have to

concentrate all her energy of the journey. Leading me away from the cleared path, she pointed out brambles and logs to be weary of, nodding or grunting when I didn't pick up the hand signal and stumbled behind her.

"For somebody with ten years of swamp critters swimming around in your veins, you sure are lousy navigating through the marsh." We had come to a small clapboard shack set out in a clearing of trees. Outside she had a fire pit and a tub of water, a clothesline strung up from a tree to the side of the building, a collection of dried out logs, and, peeking from the back of the makeshift home, some empty cages and traps. Colorful bottles were ties up to the lower hanging branches. A few chickens pecked around the dirt for whatever bugs or seedlings were there to consume. "But I s'pose flora and fauna have their different essences about 'em. It's hard to learn 'em both, I reckon."

Whomever this woman was, she seemed to know an awful lot about me—what I did, when I'd come here—compared to the nothing I knew of her. She held open her door and ushered me inside. "We'll talk in here. Away from the ears. What's the matter with you anyway? You ain't said a single word yet. Don't tell me you're a mute. That's gonna make this lots times harder."

"Who are you?"

"Oh shit," she turned red. "All this time out here and I've forgotten my basic manners. Name's Maybelle. The folks in town call me May, or the May Witch, or the Crazy Lady, if they call on me at all. When they're not scared to speak my name." She smiled slyly, amused, it seemed, by the whole thing.

"And you live out here? Alone?"

"For now on forty years, it seems. Ever since... Did you get that picture?"

She said the word like "pitcher," holding out her hand for me to offer it up to her. I pulled it from my pocket—I'd brought it with me in case Duke had figured on searching my place while I was out—and she snatched it away and studied it in the light blazing from the oil lamps she'd lit up when we'd entered.

"You left me this?"

"No, but a friend did."

"Why?"

She dropped the photograph on her table. I watched it slide down next to jars filled with liquids of various colors, next to chicken feet and dried plants and what looked like the pickled remains of some creature I had never encountered.

"Somebody leaves you a snapshot of your boy helper and that kid what turned up dead outside of Grayson's two weeks back, and you can't figure on the why? What sort of dribble did they teach you in those Floridian schools?" She pointed to both of the boys in the photographs, tapping her fingers on each face in rapid succession as if goading them to speak. "Two boys turn up at the wrong end of the beatin' stick within a few weeks of each other, then there turns up a picture of the two of them cohooting together, and you don't think there might be a connection between the both of those events?"

She sighed and placed the photo back in my hands, turning toward the table and pulling down a shallow white bowl. Gracefully, she paced to her door, swung it open and reached down to grab a rooster by the neck, jerking him upward in one fell swoop to severe the vertebrae in his neck. She pulled a knife from a drawer and spilled the rooster's innards onto the white bowl. Letting the body drop to the floor, her fingers began to massage around the entrails.

"Look here," she said. "There are two types of knowledge out there. At least two types. There's that stuff that you learn from the books and the doctors like yourself and the schools, and then there's the stuff that the world itself has to tell you. Most folks, they gonna savor one over the other. Hold it up like it's more valuable or correct. But truth is that often times neither one of them alone is gonna get you the stuff you need to know.

"The swamp is angry. Has been for some time. Poison dripping into her. Blood being shed. This ain't ominous or nothing, but it's all coming to a head. I mean, something or 'nother is always coming to a head, but this time right here for us is a major something and it seems like you're plum dab in the middle of it."

Her fingers continued to poke through the bloody organs of the rooster, separating them out and aligning them along the bowl. She seemed mesmerized by their patterns.

"Before the week is out there will be another dead. There ain't nothing that can stop that. It's already in the workings. But also there's Duke, locking you up in a cell as a scapegoat, and that there you can do something about."

"Duke's going to arrest me?"

"He's gonna try."

"Why are you helping me?"

Maybelle's eyes broke away from the bowl and she turned to

study me as she wiped her hands off on her skirt tails. She cocked her head to the side briefly then went about cleaning up the mess she'd just made.

"I just don't want to see no one else get hurt," she said. "This thing what's at work here, it's old. Older than this town, even. It's been here all this time, mutating with the waters and the algae and the moss. Getting itself tangled up and turned around, and now it's 'bout to leap outward and consume a lot more than just that rich kid and Marty and you if you ain't careful. These waters have secrets they swallow down, but everything that sinks in this trembling earth makes its way back up to the surface somehow or other. You just be wary on who it is you trust and what secrets you start hearing."

Duke was waiting for me as I steered the airboat back toward my dock. He hoisted himself up from the folding chair on my back porch and began to make his way down toward the water. I did my best to discretely stow the photograph away within some of the blankets and netting folded up at my feet before he made it to the dock and reached out to help me tether the boat in place.

"Twice in one day," I said as the propeller blades slowed to a halt, the engine quieting enough to make it so I didn't have to yell. "Did your boys find anything on the pass through my place?"

"I'm afraid I can't be discussing none of that with you."

"Official investigation and all."

"No. No, because I have to place you under arrest."

I stood with my jaw hanging down, halfway between the boat and dry land. Duke glanced around the yard before letting his eyes come back to me. His handcuffs swung loosely in his fingers.

"You're not going to make me use these, are you, son?" he asked, lowering his voice even more as our ears adjusted to the silence left from the boat's engine dying. "I'd like it if you could just make this whole thing easy."

"What are the charges? What did I do?"

"Look, Marty's story done changed. Rick said Marty remembered everything this afternoon, said he must have blocked it out before due to the trauma of you coming at him with a scalpel and knocking him out."

"And why would I do that?"

"Marty says he caught you selling off ketamine to that boy in the Trans Am. Says he was coming in to confront you about it, and, I'm quoting here, you 'didn't like none what you heard.'"

"Duke, you know that's not true."

He jangled his cuffs out before him, steeled his jaw line as best he could, and looked straight into my eyes.

"Sheriff Bellows," he corrected me. "And I don't have any inkling whether what that boy and his father said is true or not. What I do know is that Rick went to the same high school as I did. That his son's going there now. And that you appeared here nine, ten years back with a government badge and a healthy dose of animal medications at your hip. So now, son, you want to try to tell me what I know and don't know again, or you wanna come with me peacefully?"

Whether it was true or not, Duke told me he'd frozen my assets on account of the investigation. He said he had to look into my finances to see if there was any extraneous money coming and going that could be traced back to the illicit sale of drugs. He told me he'd set bail low enough, should anybody I know care to get me out of here, but seemed to be laughing at the prospect of that ever happening. I'd been here ten years and aside from the occasional drink with the men down at Grayson's, many of whom still called me "Vet" instead of by name, I'd not made any what'd be called real friends. I figured it was just as much my fault as it was the xenophobic fear that inundated the locals. Ever since leaving my adoptive parents and bungling from town to town along the Gulf Coast, I'd learned that attachment and transitive did not really mesh well and had stayed pretty reserved in my day-to-days. Duke would probably find a way to hold that against me.

He'd taken the keys to my place and given them to Rick—Marty, he'd said, was too traumatized to go back in—so he could feed the dogs kenneled up and give them back to their owners when they returned from the beach and remembered to come by and collect them. He said it like he was trying to be nice, like he was affording me some courtesy, but his voice was letting me know that it was more for the animals than it was for me. Sue, he said, would have to make due for herself. He spent most of the morning talking at me, with me sitting on a cotton mattress that barely hid the springs of the folding cot and him towering in the open door of the cell. It was probably a frightening sight when he was younger, him staring down whatever petty criminal he'd brought in with the light from the window behind him outlining his quarterback frame. But his weight had shifted, rounded out his middle, sagged his jowls and thinned his hair. It wasn't Duke that was making the situation feel overwhelming at all.

As soon as Duke had slammed shut the cell door, Charles huffed over and laid down to guard it, looking at me with his forlorn hound eyes, and trying to keep his ears from resting underneath his paws. I crossed to sit on the floor beside him, reached through the bars and absently rubbed the scruff around his haunches. I couldn't shake what Maybelle had said. She'd told me I'd be arrested before the week was out, and it had come true. Did that mean that everything she'd predicted would? Was there going to be another death by week's end?

I was trying to put Maybelle and her swamp voodoo out of my mind when Deputy Squalls entered the cellblock from the offices and processing areas. Charles barely acknowledged the man before licking my extended fingers once more and trotting out of the room. Squalls had vaguely Native American features, crisp black hair and tanned skin, a pronounced nose and prominent forehead that he kept hidden most times by his county-issued hat. Whereas most folks around Southern Georgia were at peace with or had forgotten all about that one-sixteenth Indian bloodline, Squalls was reminded of it daily. His grandfather had changed the family surname from McArthur to Squalls, and I couldn't tell if the deputy's attempts at masking his heritage were in response to his father running off to a reservation or an actual shame he had kindled within himself.

"You're free to go," Squalls said, unlocking the cell door, but not opening it yet as I got to my feet. He grasped my hand between the bars and pressed his face against them, lowering his voice to whatever's less than a whisper. "Even a kind man who is hungry will find himself dining with wolves. Be wary."

Squalls led me out of the cellblock to find Holton Martin tapping his toes in one of the waiting area chairs. Holt hopped to his feet when I entered, and Squalls left to collect the envelope with my belongings.

"Duke 'n his boys are still fine-tooth combing over that place of yers," Holt informed me, as if this, his bailing me out, should have made complete sense to me. "How 'bout we go on out to Grayson's and have ourselves some swill up 'til we can get you back in your own grounds?"

"You bailed me out?"

"'Tweren't much. I like to help folks. Just as long as you don't go jumpin' out on yer court date so as I get my money back, I reckon there ain't no harm done. Or hell, even if you do jump out on it, I's prolly gonna die soon anyhows, so it's really no loss on either count."

Squalls handed me a manila envelope with my wallet, shoelaces, and belt. They'd let me keep on my own clothes seeing as how I hadn't officially been booked yet since they couldn't find any actual evidence. I looped my belt around me and shoved my wallet back into my pocket before following Holt out to the parking lot. He led me to a brand new pickup, green, mostly, with a wide white stripe down the side and an extra large truck bed, and motioned for me to hop in on the passenger side.

"Like I said," Holt motioned to the vehicle as we both climbed into the cab, "I figure I could go at any minute and I might as well live it up while I'm still 'round. There ain't no tellin' what the other side offers, and Colt has never been one to offer up any stories."

"Did you do this on your own volition?" I asked, feeling silly even as the words came out of my mouth. Duke cocked his head to look at me from the corner of his right eye, keeping the left one trained on the road ahead as we made our way out to Grayson's. "I mean, nobody asked you to do this, did they?"

"Who out there would ask me to get yer ass out of jail, boy?"

I stammered. I wasn't sure what I should tell Holt. Twice today I'd been warned about trusting people. But Holt had just pulled me out of custody and seemed harmless enough in his relentless need to help. "I was just wondering if maybe Maybelle put you up to it."

Holt's face turned cold as stone, his jaw twisted roughly and he hocked loudly as he spit from the open window. His eyes froze and squinted on the horizon line. He kept his face trained forward.

"Don't no need to be speaking that woman's name," Holt spat. "Don't you go getting mixed up with her. All her crazy can seep right into yer brain."

I had never seen that sort of vile hatred drip from Holt's usually jovial demeanor. He barreled down the road for a half-mile or so before he could shake it off. The sparkling glint usually evident in his eyes returned and he smiled at me with the corner of his mouth. His hands released their death grip on the steering wheel and the color returned to his knuckles.

"Ain't nothin' a swig of Arnold's old rotgut can't take care of," Holt chuckled. "No matter how long a body's in a cell, it can creep in and turn him dark. You need a bit of darkness to swish it on out."

The men crowded into Grayson's all went silent as Holt and I walked in. Eyes darted as quickly as they could from me to the tops of their glasses, watching the caramel color of their beer or whiskey rock inside. It was obvious that they'd heard about my arrest, or if not, about Marty's trip to the hospital and had pegged me as a villain already. I sucked in a deep breath and followed Holt up toward the bar, taking a seat on the stool next to him and nodding as Neal poured out two fingers, neat for Holt and then mine on the rocks with a splash of water. That was another nod to my foreignness, the splash of water. No matter how many times I asked, Neal reckoned my stomach couldn't handle the local swill without something to cut it.

"Here's to truth and trust and justice, and all that other shit that makes us proud to be men 'round these parts." Holt clinked his glass against mine and sucked down a hefty gulp. He motioned for Neal to keep them coming, and the two of us sat in silence as the hum of conversation returned to the bar. I heard my name whispered amidst the general din through the first few drinks, but before long it seemed the talk had moved beyond my perils to whatever ins and outs the wives were getting up to, the size of the latest catches on the St. Mary's versus those from the Suwannee, or the "did you get a gander of that latest bride hightailing it down the street outside the courthouse, that tuxed-up fucker chasing her down like she was worth the alimony payments after the years of yakking and yard work."

Holt stayed quiet the entire time. His eyes were darting from my fingers to my eyes and back each time I pulled the highball to my lips as if he were studying my features in hopes of some glimmer of recognition to spring forward. The noise of the late evening crowd inside Grayson's washed over us in waves, ebbing and flowing, filling my ears and then evacuating to a near deafness before hitting again. The whole motion of it—the undulations of sound and light as the door opened to admit new revelers, the sparks as cigarettes lit up shining like foxfires throughout the room, even as it seemed to be growing increasingly darker—heightened the buzz I was feeling from the alcohol seeping from my stomach into my bloodstream. I felt dizzy waves of exhaustion. Neal's pappy's moonshine, which I'd been so sure I could handle, was knocking through my gut, taking the wind out of me with each sip. I had to focus on my breath, attempting to regulate my inhalations so it did not seem as if I was gasping like a trout reeled in and still dangling from the hook. Each time I closed my eyes it seemed to take longer to spring them back open.

"You 'right there, boy?" Holt asked me. I barely caught the concerned look on his face as he leaned closer to me in slow motion, even as my eyelids blacked out the scene.

I smelled the mildew even before the sounds, muffled and dank, found their way into my consciousness. My back was against a hard surface, my arms down to my side. At first I worried that I'd fallen from the barstool at Grayson's, but something didn't feel right. The flooring wasn't wood. Instead, it felt like compacted, hard clay, smoothed from years of wear, cold to the touch. People moved around me in a hurried fashion, as if preparing for something important. A gut instinct told me to keep my eyes closed, to stop the reflex flutter of eyelashes as my body attempted to regain control of itself.

"You think he's coming to?"

"Nah. He'll be out for at least the night. What with what we gave him."

"You sure he's going to play into this?"

"He won't have much of a choice. Besides which, it's the best way to make sure he goes all in."

The voices sounded so familiar. Faces and names floated through my blurring brain, nearly surfacing and then diving back into the deeper recesses of my mind. I felt like I should jump up and scream, call the practical joke and be on my way. I had no idea where I could be, how many men were moving around me. I decided to risk it and attempt at opening my eyes, if for nothing else than to get my bearings.

Wherever I was, it was bright. The sudden glare snapped my eyelids shut.

I had made out three men, at least. I wasn't sure if these were the two I'd heard speaking before or not. Each of them seemed clad in a dark shirt and dark pants, though it was possible my mind was simply attempting to fill in the glimpsed vision with blackened silhouettes. For the first time since finding out I'd been adopted, I felt helpless. It rolled over me like wind in the fields, threatening to double me over. It seemed as if a second wave of drunkenness was taking hold.

"We gone teach you yet how to hold yer liquor," Holt guffawed. "You were mumbling all kinds of craziness in yer sleep there, boy. Stuff about dark men in black robes like you was dreamin' 'bout some satanic cult stuff. You ain't no devil worshipper, is you?"

My head was swirling as I tried to lift myself up to my elbows and take in my surroundings. I must've been at Holt's place; I didn't recognize anything in the room. There were two small twin beds, separated by a nightstand, like the set of a 1960s sitcom where the husband and wife couldn't be shown to sleep together. The wall was wood-paneled—it looked like oak, but was probably imitation, clapboard covered with a "realistic wood" stickering—and covered with taxidermied fish and commemorative plates. The overhead lights from the ceiling fan were hurting my eyes, causing me to squint as the light danced from the twirling blades to create a strobing effect across my face, and I tried to keep my stomach from churning as I glanced around for a lamp to lessen the daze I was experiencing. There wasn't one. Holt was fully dressed, sitting on the edge of the opposite bed and cocking his head slightly to the left as he studied my own body coming to. My shirt was missing, as were my shoes, but I still had my pants, belt, wallet, and socks on me.

"That bed there was meant for Colt, when he decides he's done playing out there in the muck and needs a softer headrest. But he ain't been here in so long I reckoned he weren't none to show up last night. You think you can handle some breakfast?"

Holt showed me to his john and had toast and bacon set out when I emerged, still reeling from the moonshine we'd consumed the night before. He seemed chipper, not affected at all by the swill, and I sat down at the table timidly, my mind grasping to reclaim any memory of passing out or leaving Grayson's. Holt poured me some milk that he said would help my stomach and sat down across from me to eat.

"You gave me a fright, bud," Holt said, scraping butter across a piece of toast. The sound of the knife moving over the charred bread echoed through my eardrums. "You tore out of Grayson's so fast last night I thought the ghost of some ol' Injun took hold of yer body. 'Course we both know that weren't the spirit what got into you.

"I found you wandering out on the roadside, 'bout to fall flat in a ditch to sleep. Yer shirt all bloodied up like you'd gotten yerself banged up, but I didn't see no wounds once I got you back here. I prolly got a shirt that'll fit you though. So you don't have to get home all bare-chested."

I was mostly silent as we went through breakfast, but Holt

We Tremble As We Sink

took over the conversation, attempting to fill in the night for me. I couldn't remember any of it, it seemed. When I'd managed to get down a half slice of toast and most of the milk, Holt offered to drive me back over to my place. He gave me a trash bag with the bloody shirt I couldn't remember bloodying up and a clean shirt from his closet to put on. He tossed my boots to me, and I got dizzy again watching them fly through the air, then again unsteady as I bent down to slide them on and tie the laces.

Sheriffs' cars were pooling in my driveway as Holt's pickup drove near. He slowed to a stop a ways up the road, giving the two of us a chance to survey the scene to try to figure out what was going on. I pulled my head in from the open window, the idling vehicle no longer making me want to hurl, and watched as Holt quietly grabbed the trash bag stuffed with my bloodied shirt and pushed it beneath the seat. Duke's sedan was one of the cars; I recognized the license plate. Holt eased into the driveway and parked in the grass away from the patrol cars. We both stepped out tentatively, looking around to see where the Sheriff and his deputies were, walking slowly as much for my headache as for taking in the scene. I glanced toward the dug out pond and noticed Sue doing her best to hide just below the water's surface, shy but annoyed at her afternoon sunbathing being disrupted.

Holt called out for Duke, and Deputy Squalls rounded the corner from the backyard. His eyes avoided mine as he moved quickly to meet us.

"Holt, you should just turn right around and head out of here," he said, eyeing the ground for a moment before his pupils finally rested on mine. "Duke wants to see you, since you're here."

"I'll be at my place if you need anything," Holt nodded to me. He shook Deputy Squall's hand and began to make his way back toward his truck.

Squalls immediately darted his eyes away from my face, trying desperately for anywhere else to look. He turned and began walking slowly back around the house, motioning for me to follow. Holt's truck cranked up behind us, and I could hear Duke yelling obscenities from around the other side of the house. The peace I'd felt on my property only a few days ago had vanished. Now the swamp seemed to be rising forth, doing its damnedest to suck all the oxygen from the air, to block out the sky. Squalls stopped just shy of the corner, the two of us tight against the frame of the house so I

37

could not see around.

"You may want to brace yourself before we go 'round," he warned me. "Or, if Duke's right, there ain't no need." His eyes found mine again. "Just remember what I told you at the station."

Four men in uniform were standing with Duke about fifteen paces from my back porch. They all had their hands on their hips, heads still, and feet together; posing like superheroes against the sharp afternoon sun dancing through the humidity that swelled the closer you got to the water. Another deputy in plastic gloves with clear evidence bags was combing over my airboat, and I was sure I could hear a few more moving about inside my house.

"Afternoon, Sheriff Bellows," I called out, suddenly emboldened and determined to see a warrant for the search they were conducting.

Duke turned to face me, his jowls quivering and sweat drenching his forehead. That's when I noticed it. A six-foot long mound of white situated behind the Sheriff and his cronies. A body. In my backyard. The white sheet they'd used to cover it while awaiting the coroner to show up was beginning to attract flies and other insects, and it seemed like one of the deputy's sole responsibility was shooing them away. Afraid to approach the body, he planted his feet several paces away from the fabric that, I could see now, had small patches of blood soaked into it near what seemed to be the shoulder, hip, and ankle regions of the corpse. The deputy leaned forward from the knee and blew at the bugs, swishing his hands through the air to keep them from alighting on the sheet. When he'd turn his head away from the body to breathe in a deep breath before turning back to exhale on the insects, I had to force back a laugh caused either by the comical scene of the deputy or the tension that clung to the air like gnats, I wasn't sure which.

Duke's eyes tightened as he studied my face. "Only a few hours out, and what have you been getting into?"

"What's going on here?"

"Why don't you tell me," Duke demanded. He clenched his teeth and slammed his fist against his other palm for emphasis. "All I know is, you get out of my cell–"

"I was only in, and unjustly at that, for a few hours."

"–You get out of my cell and suddenly I got myself another dead boy turned up in your backyard. And you nowhere to be seen."

I thought about what Holt told me, about turning up roadside with a bloodied shirt and no memory. I wondered if I could have gone home, found someone breaking in, and turned a scalpel on him. I wondered if I had that in me. Duke seemed to notice the fear in my face.

"Who is it?" I asked.

"I'm asking the questions."

I stammered for a moment, sure then that it wasn't anyone we knew, or else Duke would have put that out there. He seemed just as unsure of the scenario as I was.

"I was with Holt all night," I said. "We were at Grayson's. There'd be witnesses."

"I know you was there," Duke's eyes seemed to sparkle as he spoke. "And I also know you was drunk off your ass on Arnie's ol' moonshine. And that you up and tore out of that place like some demon ghost done possessed you, and Holt had to go out looking for your sad, pathetic ass."

"You think I killed whoever that is? Why would I?"

"I reckon maybe your drunk ass comes up to your place in the middle of the night and you find this guy rambling through your backyard. Maybe he's lost, some out of town kid whose car broke down. Or maybe he's trying to break in and rob the place. And then maybe you don't like that and you go at him like you went at Marty. Only this guy doesn't faint so you slash him with your blade and leave him there for your handicapped gator to take care of. Rogers finds him this morning when he comes 'round to give the Dayton's back their dog, and you ain't nowhere near."

"I was with Holt," I repeated. "He found me wandering down the road and took me back to his place to sober up."

The coroner had arrived to collect the body, and Duke escorted me around to the side of the house, determined not to let me see the body should I notice something that could help me in any way. He seemed to have formed a personal vendetta against me. The deputy who had been searching my boat approached, the smile on his face resembling that on Duke's. His nametag read "Bellows."

"This was shoved underneath the seat, Dad."

The deputy handed Duke a plastic bag with the photograph that showed Marty and the first body, the one from the Trans Am crash, back when it was still alive and breathing. Duke seemed more shocked by the picture than by the compilation of bodies that seemed to be turning up throughout the bogs. He looked from the photo to me.

"This, sir, does not look good for you."

The body had been loaded into the coroner's black van, and the deputies had begun to mill around near their vehicles, looking for the signal from Duke that they could leave. Duke held my eyes in his, attempting to stare me down.

"You questioned Marty?" I asked, attempting bold and indignant, but hearing my voice warble. "He obviously knew that Burt kid."

"I should take you in again."

"We don't have any evidence. It'd be the same deal as last time, with Judge Dixon turning him loose within the hour."

I hadn't even noticed Squalls approaching us. He nodded to me subtly, and I let my gaze return to Duke's. "Don't leave town," he warned me and rounded up his men to finally give me some peace.

I paced through my backyard, absently searching for anything the deputies may have missed that could help me piece together what had happened. I tried to make sense of any of it. Holt had told me he posted bail, but Squalls had said a judge had released me for lack of evidence. But then Holt had hidden my bloodied clothing. For the life of me, I could not figure out why. The sky was beginning to darken as the last rays of sunshine poured through the trees. I stopped my meandering gait and studied the dried blood pooled on the flattened grass where the body had lain. A soft, evening rain began to fall, tiny drops of water splashing against the red and green in my blurring vision.

Behind me, Sue let out a hungered roar, and I turned to see her pulling herself along the yard, her eyes weak and frightened and angry. I realized I had not fed her since the previous morning and quickly shook out of my daze to put the beef I'd been thawing in the refrigerator on my back porch for her. Her massive jaws locked over the meat, dragging it off to eat in peace while I sat down on the steps of my porch and ignored the rain that began to quicken as the night descended. My stomach growled, and I pushed through the perturbation at entering my house. I ate quickly and pulled myself into the shower, attempting to wash the day off of me, willing it to end.

My mind raced as the water flowed around me, it pooled at my feet fighting against the slow moving drain of my tub. I could not remember anything outside of the dream I'd had the night before. I could not picture myself, scalpel in hand, butchering the body of some young Floridian boy who was stumbling and lost on my property. I thought of his parents sitting on the sofa in their A-frame down near St. Petersburg. His mother knitting or crocheting something to keep her hands busy while his father downed a beer, empty cans pooling at his feet, the news reports from the television droning on into an endless string of syllables, barely audible and not at all understood. Their little boy gone. Forever.

Except they weren't his parents, they were mine. My adoptive mother and father. And me, a twelve year old boy sitting on the floor behind the couch and firing toy guns at the cat who would chase after the nylon balls and bat them around the linoleum floor of the kitchen before losing them beneath the stove. I felt alone and invisible. Standing in the shower, those feelings launched over me once more. I remembered I had just found the papers, the ones concerning my adoption. I remembered just finding out my life had been a lie.

I was snooping through my parents' bedroom while they were both out; my mom at the grocery store or yarn store or driving her car between them, my dad still at work at whatever job he'd not been fired from that week. I was looking for something. A birthday present, maybe, or my father's porn collection, attempting to suss out the hiding places they used when I found the box of old report cards and legal documents. And my adoption papers. I hadn't told them yet that I knew. I put the box back exactly where I'd found it and spent the next weeks trying to be unnoticed. I remember being afraid that if I told them, they'd know I'd been searching through their private belongings. I remember fearing my father's leather belt.

A commercial began extolling the virtues of a weekend at Busch Gardens and my father grumbled as he rose to his feet. He kicked the aluminum cans piled up on the carpet and stomped into the kitchen to retrieve another beer. The cat dove across the floor in pursuit of the ball I'd just fired. Dad's boot stomped down, then kicked the poor feline's body violently against the legs of the kitchen table. He barely even noticed as he grabbed a beer and returned to his throne. I scooped up the cat and rubbed her ribs. She seemed in a daze, but quickly shook it off and dove again toward the nylon bullet still resting on the floor. It must have been then that I first thought about becoming a veterinarian. It must have been then that I first considered leaving.

I turned the faucet off and stepped out of the shower, suddenly aware of noises circling through the vents. It sounded like people were moving through the rooms of my house. I thought I could hear voices. Quickly, I pulled on the clothes I had been wearing before bathing and quietly slipped from the bathroom. Holt stood at the end of the hallway, framing the doorway into my living room.

"We heard what happened," he said. "We're here to help."

There were five of them total, inside my house, standing near the furniture as if at any moment they were prepared to sit, to become informal, but none of them ever did. It was as if their bodies were all trapped in the limenal space between the friendly circle offering out a helping hand of justice and something darker, more sinister. I pictured them all in black robes chanting in some dead language that did its best to incorporate the slow lilt of a southern dialect with mispronounced Greek, misused Latin, some Native languages littered throughout. My fevered, drunken dream from the night before was clouding into my waking life.

But they weren't dressed any differently than they normally were. Holt had on the same thing he'd dropped me off in earlier. He'd combed his white hair over the balding space at his crown, but otherwise was the same Holt. Donna Michaels, the woman who owned the yarn store in the Piggly Wiggly shopping center, had on a floral print dress with long sleeves, even in this heat, and a white lace collar that was buttoned all the way up, despite the strain it seemed to be putting on her neck. Peter Nichols was in overalls, shifting from foot to foot and glancing down periodically to make sure he wasn't tracking any mud from his work-boots onto my floor. I wasn't acquainted with the other two, not enough to know their names. But I thought I recognized the man from Grayson's—I was sure I'd seen him there a few times—and the woman, whom I assumed to be his wife from the way they were crowding near to one another—had a genuineness about her eyes that started to lull me if I looked at her for too long.

Holt did most of the talking.

"There's stuff about the swamp, 'bout livin' here and breathin' in the air and the insects, 'bout sucking down the water and walking on the soil, that gets terrifying. It's hidden, most of it, inside of the tranquility the heat and humidity push down through us. Like it wants to keep a lid on things, keep something suppressed. It's pushing down so hard on our eyelids that it keeps 'em half-shut to what's actually at work. The nightmares that got filtered through the bogs and come out screaming if we ain't lucky enough.

"That's what's happenin' now, best we can tell. The bad shit's done found it's way up and come hollering out to catch up with us.

Like Duke. He ain't really a bad guy. Just a man trying to do his job. But he's done got two bodies on his hands and he's looking for a scapegoat and that's where you come in. That's what we're thinkin' anyway. That's why as we want to help."

I pushed further into my living room, taking a seat on the couch. My guests, the self-proclaimed saviors who'd let themselves into my house, all adjusted their stances to keep me centered within their circle. Their faces held looks of sympathy, like they were coddling a toddler who'd just got his first glimpse of the cruelty of living.

"Think about those cypress trees out there. They're all hundreds of years old. They know this place, know what it offers. They've figured out a means to stand tall and firm in the still waters. The bases of their trunks balloon out to give 'em balance. Their roots hold the soil in place, keep it from eroding. They want to work with the system. And then their limbs get all muddled up with Spanish moss. Sagging 'em down. Spanish moss is a parasite, latching on, burring its roots right into the soft wood of those trees, sucking out the nutrients. That's the thanks the swamp gives those trees. The cypress hold the earth together and the swamp gives 'em leeches as a reward. What I'm sayin' is, the dark is always there. Sometimes it's just more evident than others."

Everyone seemed to be waiting for me to speak, or nod, or give some sign of encouragement.

"I don't understand what this has to do with these dead kids and bodies piling up in my yard. I don't get why I need your help at all, or why you want to offer it to me."

"You seem like a good man." This was Donna Michaels speaking. She held her hands clasped in front of her pelvis and spoke with an upward lilt to her voice, like she'd been straining her vocal cords for years to speak in an higher octave that left her breathy. "You don't have no real people in your life though. Ten years here and still an outsider. But that's just how it goes around these parts. You came here to tend to the swamp. To take care of the animals in it. And you didn't forget about the people here either. Took in and cared for their beasts all the same. So when the swamp tries to spit you out, we want to help you make it through. It only seems right and neighborly."

"Look," Holt said, crossing to me and resting his calloused palm on my shoulder, "we're part of a group that understands these wetlands. We know the vile and the vitriol that gurgle up from the depths, but we also know the beauty that is inherent in this land. Our pappies and our mamas were all part of it. It's tradition, passed on down and cherished. We got connections. We got ways. We can help you, if you want our help."

I let my eyes focus on the leg of the couch across the room, and Holt's hand fell from my shoulder. I tried to take in what he was telling me; to imagine a secret society of swamp-worshippers meeting clandestinely at night behind the strip mall to ensure the habitat remained neutral to the muck and the mire. It was laughable. And now five of them, descended down through the generations, were standing in my living room, offering me help in clearing my name for a murder I didn't commit.

"I didn't do nothing wrong," I said. "There won't be any evidence against me, none that says I killed that kid."

"It don't matter none," Holt shot back. "That's what we're trying to get you to see. The swamp is rising up, swallowing us down. Or else we're sinking. Either way, it's coming to take hold of things and it's got Duke by the heels. And he'll move Hell and high water to take somebody down for this. And it's looking most suited to let that somebody be you. Duke don't understand when the quag is taking hold. Neither did his daddy. Or his granddaddy. Duke talks a big game 'bout his family going back for generations in these parts, but none of 'em, not a single one of 'em ever really understood it. We can help you because we got that on our side. Our knowing. Our knowhow. And we got others. You'd be surprised who else 'round here is with us on this. Friends. That's what we are. Judge Dixon what got you out of jail, he gets it. And we think you see it too."

Holt told me he'd heard from friends that the boy whose body had turned up in my backyard was a drug dealer from the Pensacola region of Florida, that he'd had a few priors when he was seventeen or eighteen and then had dropped off the map for about two years only to turn up here, dead. Killed. When Holt said "Friends" now, I heard it with the capital F like that. As if the friends in question were part of his secret cult. I imagined half the town traipsing in their skivvies through the backwaters, rejoicing in the wonder of the land. I was doing all I could to hold back the laughter that was gurgling up inside of me.

In two days' time I'd gone from being the local veterinarian to the Sheriff's top murder suspect. I'd met a swamp witch and been tossed in jail and gotten railed off my ass on moonshine. I'd dreamed about a cult of devil-worshippers and now five crazy swamp devotees were standing in my living room offering their help on quelling the murder charge through their understanding of the bog. It was all too much to take. I expected the hazing ritual to be over at any moment. For Duke to burst from the shadows with a "gotcha!" and a hearty handshake to welcome me, finally, after ten years, to the community. I felt delirious. I felt numb. I needed sleep.

But sleep did not come easy, even hours after the group had pulled away from my driveway and left me to consider their offer of unknown aid. When the sun began flashing through the blinds on my window, I felt as if my eyes had barely closed once throughout the night. Still, I pulled myself to my feet and trudged into the kitchen to put on the coffee. As the pot began to hiss and steam, I wandered outside to pull Sue's lunch from the freezer to give it time to thaw out. I tossed the cut of meat into my kitchen sink and poured myself a cup of coffee. It burned my tongue, but seemed to be doing the trick as it hit my stomach. My eyes locked on the thawing beef, glazing as I focused on the condensation forming on the plastic wrap, blurring the red musculature below. I could trace the separations in the muscles, in the bone, that the butcher had made in the cow. I remembered the large animal focus of my veterinary school, slicing through a bull's thick skin. How similar the butcher and the vet were in their understanding of the beasts.

I knew Sue would probably have preferred freshly killed meals, but I couldn't afford the cost. And she seemed happy enough, cut off from the dangers that had removed her leg as a young gator, with her own pond and daily meals. And she genuinely seemed to like my companionship. I appreciated hers. Sue was the only creature since I'd moved here who didn't seem to have an issue with me. Sue was–Sue was hungry!

She had practically begged for food when I'd returned home the previous afternoon. She had not attempted to dine on the bloody body lain across my lawn. If the murder had really occurred on site the previous night, Sue would have had ample time to find and devour parts of the body. She had not eaten for over a day, what with me in jail and then drunk at Holt's. The body would have had to been placed there just before Deputy Rogers arrived to give the Dayton's back their hound. More than likely someone who knew Rogers would be coming. Someone–not the swamp or its rising or our sinking–was trying to set me up for the murder of that kid.

I drove into town, parked my pickup in front of the courthouse and wandered down the sidewalk with no particular destination in mind. I needed a distraction, and maybe a drink, but didn't think Grayson's would be the best place to go. I was more afraid of running into Holt, of having to give him an answer on his cult's proffer of assistance than of the potential for running into Duke or his deputies there. I was met by awkward glances, rushed eyes flashing away to seem busy or uninterested with every storefront I passed. Or else I was given a sort of knowing nod, telling me Holt's secret society was not all that great at keeping their own secret.

The newspapers glaring at me from the fifty-cent bins along the strip featured the mugshot of the boy who'd been found in my backyard. He was young—younger in the photo than he'd been at death as he'd not had any run-ins with the law in about two years—but the skin around his eyes looked haggard and worn. It was easy to picture Duke's tale of the murder: the boy—Mario Hernandez—prowling the local vet's office for drugs to push at the Florida nightlife. A drunken me, stumbling upon him, defending my property. The paper didn't mention me, thankfully, but it was obvious the gossip hounds had been yipping over the clotheslines.

I was about to give up on finding a peaceful drink downtown when Charles came bumbling across the street to me, tripping over his ears as he padded across the asphalt. Duke was a few paces behind his dog, the cold demeanor draped across his face making him seem larger and older than he was. He raised his palm for me to stop where I was.

"Where'd you hide the scalpel?" he asked, not losing a moment to any pleasantries. "The one you sliced up that boy with? I'll dredge the fucking waters behind your house if need be, son, so you might as well make this easier on all of us. Hell, if you cooperate, they'll be more likely to go easy on you, seeing as how you was just protecting your land and that Mario boy had more shit pumping through his system than they stock at Goldman's pharmacy. 'Course you wanna know what I'm thinking now? I'm thinking he weren't no stranger to you. I'm thinking you knew him from when you lived over there. And now he's all growed up and you're thinking you can make some extra cash by hocking your medicines on the side as party favors. Then the deal goes south. That's what I'm thinking now. And I'm thinking he weren't the first one. That that kid in the Trans Am was pushing for you too. And it won't be long 'til I can prove it, so you might as well just make this easier on the both of us."

I wanted to tell Duke that he'd been watching too many cop

shows on cable, the way he was showing off and creating scenarios. He needed a fall guy, and I was as good a choice as any. Better even, if I were to believe Holt.

"Don't tell him anything."

The voice had come from behind me, stopping my words in my throat. I half-turned to see a man in his mid-thirties decked out in khakis and a navy polo shirt approaching us. He bore a determined, stern gaze and jutted his lower jaw forward inside his tight-lipped mouth, taking on a self-righteous air of import.

"What the hell are you doing here, Stephen?" Duke asked, flustered, but seemingly excited to watch the moment unfurl, as if for once, he thought, he was actually doing real detective work.

"I'm his lawyer," Stephen answered back, holding on Duke's face for his disturbed reaction before turning to hand me his card. "Holt hired me. Said you might be needing some assistance."

"Hiring a lawyer sure seems like an admission of guilt to me," Duke huffed.

"I didn't hire a lawyer. I can't afford a lawyer."

Stephen touched my shoulder, as if trying to reassure me of my innocence and his competence. "There won't be any financial burden on you," he said.

"You're taking this sucker on pro-bono?" Duke laughed.

Stephen continued to talk to me, ignoring Duke almost completely. "Why don't you stop by my office later this evening?" he asked. "The address is on the card. We can discuss everything–in private–then. Say around seven?"

I flipped the business card in my hand and slid it into my back pocket. We, the three of us, seemed to be in an unspoken standoff. Charles cowered at our feet, slumping his body even lower toward the sidewalk. Finally, I nodded. The tension in the air seemed to immediately dissipate. Duke relaxed his jaw a bit, and I saw Stephen's shoulders go slack. I bee-lined back for my truck, hopping into the cab, and watched as the two men I'd left on the sidewalk headed into the Salty Water's Tavern together, Stephen's arm slapped around Duke's shoulders and what seemed to be friendly banter passing between them.

I was not surprised to see someone waiting for me when I got home. When I rounded the corner of my house, she was sitting on the small dock beside my airboat, her own dinghy tied alongside mine. Sue was resting beside her, allowing Maybelle to caress the stump of her missing leg, being careful not to let her tail hit the waters. It was the closest I'd seen Sue to the actual swamp since I'd taken her in years prior. Maybelle seemed to have a calming effect on her. She certainly had a calming effect on me.

Maybelle waited patiently as I nodded and let myself in through the backdoor. I soon emerged with the thawed beef and tossed it out for Sue to enjoy. As she pulled herself toward her grub, I made my way to the water.

"I guess you heard," I said.

"Why don't we go for a ride?"

Maybelle used an oar to push her boat along the waterways as if we were touring the streets of Venice. She said she enjoyed the quiet of not having a motor blaring through the din of the deeper swamp. She preferred the gentle disturbance of the water to the rapid ripple of rowing. She refused to let me push us through and kept the conversation to trivial observations about our surroundings, telling me facts and figures I had learned while working for the State Park, as if she were concerned that someone around us was watching, was listening. The swamp is one of the Seven Natural Wonders of Georgia; the Okefenokee is four hundred and thirty eight thousand acres; the Suwanee River and the Saint Mary's River both originate in the swamp, with the Saint Mary's flowing out to the Atlantic and the Suwanee making its path down to the Gulf of Mexico. Maybelle smiled with each tidbit she imparted, winking at me and pointing out the wildlife—the herons and egrets and lizards and frogs—as we passed by.

She looked to be in her late fifties, perhaps, but I had a feeling she was much older than that. Her hair was just beginning to gray, and large streaks salted the stark black in a way that seemed at once regal and witchy. Her lilac-hued eyes were eager, alert with a quickness I'd only ever see before in the girls I'd dated during my days slinging drinks down the Florida coasts, that sort of light and wonder that they'd have before the alcohol really began to set in. The deeper we moved into the swamp, the more alive Maybelle seemed.

She angled the boat toward a patch of moss-covered land where Deputy Squalls stood, hands relaxed at his side, waiting patiently. He caught hold of the nose of the boat and helped pull us ashore, tying the boat in place as if he was always around to secure the woman's keel.

Squalls offered Maybelle his hand for support as we moved

further away from the water, and she took it lightly, not really needing the stability but seeming to enjoy the comfort.

"Thank you, son," she said, and I immediately saw the resemblance. Both Maybelle and Squalls had the same pronounced nose, the same hairline. Squalls had deep, near-black irises where Maybelle's were lighter, but the shape of their eyelids, the way they rested above their cheekbones, was early identical.

"You're related?" I asked, incredulous despite the similarities in their features.

"She's my mother," Squalls replied, his eyes alight with the same wonder that had filled Maybelle's as we pushed through the waters.

Squalls, it seemed, had not been the victim of a Native-obsessed grandfather, but had changed his own name in order to function in town without the stigma of the bog witch on his shoulders. Nonetheless, he was here, with his mother. And he seemed to genuinely love her.

"Don't look so surprised," Maybelle gently scolded me. "I was a fertile young woman once upon a time. Lenny, here, would've even had a big brother had the croup not taken him away as a baby. But those were different times then, those forty-odd years ago. Things were different for unmarried women holding babies in their stomachs. Lenny changed his name to Squalls, but he's a Faircloth through and through."

I watched the two as they led the way deeper onto the island. I almost envied their closeness, wondering as we clipped forward how my adoptive mother was doing, where she had been in the years since I'd spoken to her. We came upon Maybelle's little cabin, approaching it from the opposite side than we had the last time I'd been there. I saw her hens clucking and batting at the ground in search of seed beside a small pen I'd not noticed before with a sow and three suckling piglets. Maybelle cooed at them as we passed, though they took little notice of our arrival.

"How do you keep the wild animals from making off with them?" I asked, eyeing the close quarters of the dense trees around us.

"They's all wild animals," Maybelle replied. "But if you know what to offer, know how to find that balance, it all evens out. And I can have mine, and they theirs. But right now, boy, what we need to talk about is this pickle you've done found yourself in. We need to get a way of restoring that balance."

The shadows stretched, long and narrow, across the side-walk as I quickened my pace toward Stephen Thomas' office. It was only twenty past seven, and the scheduled meeting time had been 'round-about, but I did not want the man to think I was standing him up. I needed to pursue my options in case Maybelle's magic failed to work.

Deputy Squalls had given me a ride back to my place from his mother's shack in the woods. He was remarkably like the old woman now that I knew of their connection. As he pushed the boat along, he told me that Okefenokee was actually from the Hitchiti In-dian word for "land of the trembling earth." He said his ancestors on his father's side had called the place that because of the peat moss and still waters giving the impression of solid soil that broke and washed away beneath the feet of the hunters. It was imagined that one wrong step could bring the entire swamp under, that one mis-placed footstep would shake the lands so roughly that everything would be swallowed, sinking down into the underworld. He told me that Marty and his dad had come back by the station to renege on the story they'd formulated after they realized there was prob-ably no money in it. Or perhaps they'd had some change of heart at dragging a good man's name through the mud. Either way, Duke had some sort of vendetta on me and wasn't willing to let out of that new development just yet. As he spoke, my hand repeatedly rubbed the back of my head, feeling for the missing patch of hair I'd left be-hind at Maybelle's. I could still feel the bone she had used to scrape the inside of my mouth, rubbing against my cheek, collecting saliva. My fingertip throbbed slightly from the prick she'd used to collect a few drops, about a thimble full, of blood. I had not asked her what she was planning to do with it all. For some reason, I trusted her—at least more so than I felt inclined to trust Holt and his cronies. Her peace with the swamp seemed to come out of living in it, of living with it, becoming a part of the land in a way that celebrates its dark-ness and its light. Holt's group seemed to want to domesticate the grounds, to control them in some way that made them livable. Still, I found myself ringing the bell at his lawyer's front door, ready to see what they had to offer me.

Stephen's office was on the third floor of a downtown walk-up. All of the other offices were closed down for the evening. I made my way up the central staircase after he'd buzzed me in and saw him standing at the head of the stairs smiling down at me. I wasn't surprised to see Holt inside the office.

As I passed through the doorway, though, I was taken aback by the crowd packed into the room. At least thirty men and women lingered around the outskirts of the office. Donna, Peter, and the married couple who'd been with Holt in my living room the day before. Judge Dixon and several of the men who frequented Grayson's. Neal Grayson, too, and folks whose pets I knew better than their owners, along with a few faces I'd never seen before. A few young men, boys really, were huddled together near the far corner. They seemed to be uneasy, positioned on the periphery of the room, attempting, as I was, to figure out their place in it. Their sunken cheeks and the dark circles under their eyes reminded me of the two dead boys.

Stephen ushered me into the dark green leather chair opposite his desk, and as I sat down uncomfortably my fingers traced the golden brass upholstery tacks that spiraled along the seams. He offered me a drink by gesturing toward the whiskey bottles lined along the table behind his large oak desk. I shook my head and he smirked while pouring two-fingers into a highball for himself.

Holt turned to me from the identical chair beside mine. His mouth tensed as he tried to find the words, opening with a false start as he glanced around the room, then locked his eyes on mine once more.

"I've told you, briefly, about our little group," he said. His diction seemed clearer tonight, more alert, more direct. "But I obviously did not tell you everything. We needed to be sure you could be trusted, and, by showing up here tonight, we think you can be."

The faces around the room told me that not everyone was convinced, but Holt seemed to have some sort of power over them.

"The thing is: the swamp has some unique and interesting aspects that need to be preserved. And some of those assets can be very lucrative if you know how to work them. For instance, did you know that over four hundred thousand folks come traipsing in from all over the country—hell, all over the world—to camp out and boat and fish around our waters? That many people passing through, that many boats out there on the water, they're good for hiding things out in plain daylight. And we got the rivers bisecting the lands, and our waters are just muddling all right there in the inbetween, a quick and easy passage. In downright no time flat you can get a package from the coast of Mexico on up to South Carolina or even to New York.

"So what we're proposing here, what we're offering you, is that we can make all this go away—all the troubles you're having with Duke and his boys—in exchange for you opening up your office as a sort of way station for our parcels. No one's going to question a veterinarian's office being stockpiled with drugs, and we're connected enough to keep Duke's flaring nostrils away from your cabinets."

"And if I say no?"

Holt smiled. It stretched across his face like a shadow. I had never seen him look so terrifying. Two of the boys huddled together in the far corner snickered.

"If you refuse, then the fate of those two poor boys who ended up holding out on us is on your hands. And Lord knows there's enough shit out there for Duke to hold you away for years if one of us decides we want to point him in that direction."

"What Holt means," Stephen smiled from behind his desk, "is that we are prepared to extend this offer your way out of the kindness of our hearts. We don't need you so much as we need your place. You're on the water, not too far outside the Park and the town, but with enough space to make it viable. You being a doctor is a perk, but we can work around it if necessary."

"You killed those boys and now you're threatening me to join you or die?"

"Now Burt really did have an overdose what killed him," Holt resumed control of the conversation, his southern cadence returning in an attempt to put me at ease. "Your seeing that he'd been dead for longer was an unfortunate oversight on our part and got Duke to start asking questions. And Mario had been skimming off and eating half his stash. We just caught up with him in your yard that morning, or our boys there did." He nodded to the kids in the corner who seemed to grow more distant at the mention of Mario's name. "We just figured on a way to work that to our advantage. And you'll be much happier with us than against us anyway. There's money in it. And family. I know you ain't got no real family. And that's what we are. We ain't gone kill you if you say no, but we sure as hell will get you run out of town."

I sat there blankly, dumbfounded. Holt's face seemed menacing in the dim lamplight of the office. He seemed nothing like the man I'd been acquainted with weeks prior; the do-gooder with the heart of gold who put himself out for the betterment of others, constantly roaming the swamp in search of his dead brother and damsels in distress. The time he spent in the black waters, the image of a mild insanity, they made much more sense in this context. I saw in Holt's face the worst parts I'd ever imagined within my own. My finger throbbed where Maybelle had pricked it, and I felt my mouth go dry as my face flushed. I rose to my feet, and Holt let out a hearty guffaw.

"Well," he said, "I reckon we ought to give you some time to think on it all. Not that you've got much by way of options, but to give you some good faith that we're civilized folks. But you be sure that we're around. And Duke can't save you, even if you manage to overcome his crusade on your ass."

"I'm not going to Duke," I assured Holt. My eyes moved around the room, trying to remember as many faces as I could. "I just need to sleep. It feels like it's been days. Come by my place in the morning. You'll have your answer then."

Duke slipped into my house just before dawn. He'd come by water, killing the engine and rowing the last half-mile or so in case Holt or one of his boys was watching the road for vehicles and listening for the thundering of passing motorboats. I'd been unable to sleep at all and was sitting, bleary-eyed on the edge of my sofa, trying to make images out of the knots in the hardwood flooring, attempting to trick my mind into dreaming and then possibly, finally, sleep. At some point in the night I must have slept though, or slipped into some hallucinatory state of fatigue. I remembered, so vividly, parking my pickup truck in one of the spaces that lined the main drag through town, near to the courthouse and the Baptist Church.

The afternoon sun beat down, heating the sidewalk and swirling the humidity in the air to wash in waves across my face. Cars raced back and forth down the strip, tin and aluminum cans tied to their bumpers and clanging in an ever-increasing din. Three newly-wed couples stared at me from the courthouse steps, their eyes taut with anger. Behind me, a couple decked out in hiking gear, and another in fishing attire approached me rapidly. And Holt was there, orchestrating it all. The couples produced suitcases full of white powders, of vials and syringes, and tossed them into the bed of my truck, laughing as they forced me back into my cab. As I drove, I watched the cargo in my rearview. One of the cases split open, pouring blood that rapidly filled the bed and sloshed over the sides of the truck, trailing behind me on the red clay of the dirt road. Deputy Squalls stood in the road ahead of me, signaling for me to stop, but I was moving too quickly. My foot refused to find the brake. Duke stepped into the road, between Squalls and me. I was moving too fast to stop.

"You look like a wild coon's done skinned your chickens and made off with your wife." Duke was framed in the doorway by the soft haze of the morning light. He quickly pulled the door closed and circled the room to shut the blinds. "Did you get it?"

Squalls had had the idea to have me wear a tape recorder, one of those hand-held deals, not the fancy wires they used in the television shows, to my meeting with Stephen. He'd outfitted me in the water, on the boat before he dropped me off, and then gone to tell Duke what he'd done. He was confident in his mother's magic, he told me, but he thought sometimes it was necessary to use other means for the folks who didn't believe in the enchantments.

I felt around in my pocket for the recorder and noticed it propped up on the table. I rewound the cassette and pressed play for Duke. There was a muffled swishing, probably the microphone rubbing against the fabric of my clothing as I made my way up the staircase to the lawyer's office. We listened as Stephen welcomed me and ushered me into the room.

"It seems you've gotten yourself into quite the bind somehow," Stephen said. "Would you like some water?"

My eyes widened as I looked at the tape spinning through the window of the recorder. This was not the conversation we had had last night. This was not at all as I remembered it.

"Well, I just want you to know that I believe in your innocence," Stephen was saying. "Holt and I both do."

"That's right." Holt's voice was clear and precise on the recording. I could practically hear him trying to comfort me with a friendly pat on the knee.

"So why don't you tell us what happened?" Stephen coached. "When did you first notice an addiction to drugs and alcohol? If there is evidence that comes to light of your involvement in Mario Hernandez's death, we may be able to sway a judge and jury if we can get you clean and play up your sob story."

I stopped the tape. "That's not what happened."

Duke muttered obscenities to himself, his hands locked in fists inside his pockets. Arm stretched out, he clutched the recorder and jabbed it ferociously into his pocket. He wouldn't even look me in the eye as he moved toward the door. He paused briefly to glare back at me, and, in that split second, Stephen and Holt barged in.

"Any questioning of my client without me present will prove inadmissible in court," Stephen ranted, glaring directly into Duke's eyes as Holt moved to sit beside me on the couch, acting fatherly, as if he only meant comfort.

"Your client can rot in fucking hell," Duke retorted, pushing his way through the door.

I jumped to my feet to follow him, admittedly afraid to be left inside the house with these two men. They let me go, but I could feel them following, assuredly, a few paces behind. I heard Duke's truck start up as I rounded the corner of the house and watched him speed out of the drive. As the sound of his engine subsided, my eyes fell on Maybelle. She was sitting calmly on the grass, her bony fingers traversing the skin of Sue's neck. Sue had placed her body between the old woman and the house. She kept her eye trained on the old men standing behind me.

"Get yer crazy swamp ass outta here, witch," Holt called out, his voice grating, darker than usual, like the first time I'd mentioned Maybelle to him. He turned red with anger as he marched across the lawn toward the woman. She remained collected, letting her fingers work their way along Sue's spine, making no attempt to rise. Sue snapped her jaws around a dandelion blossom as Holt approached.

"Call off yer gator, boy. I swear to God I'll skin it right here in front of ya."

Maybelle rubbed the nub left by Sue's missing limb and climbed to her feet. She crossed her fingers together in front of her, turning her palms outward as if to show she was unarmed. Her breath fell evenly.

"It's been a while, hasn't it, Colt?" she asked. "Your brother around? Can I talk to him?"

"He don't none wanna talk to you, bitch. You fuckin' bog trash whore."

"Sure he does," Maybelle cooed, her palm reached out to trace the curve of Holt's jawline.

"That ain't workin' no more, harlot. Holt, Colt. Ain't no difference either way anymore. You saw to that."

Beside me, Stephen grew more and more anxious, twisting his stubby fingers first around one wrist and then the other as he paced in a small semi-circle. He pushed the sleeves to his shirt up and rolled them back down. He stumbled as his foot made contact with the grass. His eyes never left the frame of Holt's shoulders. We, Stephen and I, both watched Holt's agitation move I waves across his body, not understanding where it should be placed, seeming as confused as I was while staring onto the scene. Holt seemed like an infant, newborn and doing his damnedest to communicate something that just wasn't inside of him. At least that's how he looked from where we stood.

"Holt and I once loved each other," Maybelle was saying, her face smoothing out as best it could as she stepped closer to the old man.

"You saw to it to break him up something awful, tramp. When you went and got that baby cut out of ya, threw it off into some pig slop bucket. You broke our hearts something fierce. You can't never be forgiven for that."

Holt moved suddenly, lunging for the ax I kept sheathed next to the firewood. Stephen bolted inside, hobbling back toward my door with the vaguely spoken excuse of calling the cops. Maybelle stayed calm, even as Holt raised the blade above his shoulder to swing.

"Holt, your son is alive. Colt, tell him his son is alive."

The blade dropped to Holt's side. A wave washed over his body as his fingers released the wooden handle and the ax hit the ground. Maybelle smiled. Her eyes pushed past Holt and locked onto me briefly. I began to step forward, hoping to remove the ax from the old man's reach.

Holt sounded like himself again as he stuttered, "You had the child?"

"We weren't in no place to be parents, Holt," Maybelle said, taking his hand. "You and I, we were young and foolish, and ain't nobody alive now could say otherwise. And my Diddy, he ordered me to get rid of it. Said he was sending me to some doctor over in Tuscaloosa who did things like that. I was just a girl, and he was my dad. I told you I was getting rid of the kid, and I left town. I went to a shelter in Florida and rode out my pregnancy in that god-awful heat."

Holt was trembling. As his head turned I saw tears streaming down his face.

"It was a boy, a beautiful baby boy. He had your nose. He had your eyes. I wanted to keep him, but every time I looked at his face, all I saw was you and I couldn't take it. I signed him away there in the hospital. One of the hardest things I'd ever done. I came back here and you wouldn't have none to do with me. It was like you was a different person. And I heard you talking about Colt like he were real and here and I knew I'd done the right thing. Or the wrong thing. Either way, it was what the winds were wanting."

"Our kid is alive?" Holt repeated the phrase until it became a statement. His knees gave way beneath him.

"Holt, you gotta believe that it was the right thing to do." Maybelle turned to look at me. "You have to believe me that I did the right thing."

Seeing the two of them together, Maybelle's strong, defiant gaze never betraying her trembling lip and Holt's crumpled body heaving on the grass, my head began to spin. Their features muddled in my mind, patchworking together a baby, a young man, an adult.

The banshee scream of sirens grew loud as the gravel churned beneath Duke's wheels. I watched Holt palm the wooden handle of the ax, his fingers dipping underneath, tearing at the blades of grass as he tightened his grip on the weapon. In that moment, the thickness of the humidity-riddled air slowed everything to a sap-like crawl. I saw Sue pull herself toward the still waters; horse- and dragonflies stopped midflight to ponder the scene, to watch the muck tremble upwards. Duke's door slammed behind me. Holt's knuckles clenched and the tendons at his knees strained beneath the cotton fabric of his slacks. I dove toward the blade as he rose, already swinging the ax. The pistol held a deafening silence. Sue's tail sank beneath the black waters.

Time rushed forward in an attempt to make up for itself, to right its rotation. The barrel of Duke's gun clicked around, and my palms pushed down at the wound in Holt's shoulder. The ax lay like a discarded toy a couple of steps away on the flattened grass, only a few traces of red clay betraying the sharpness of its shine.

I yelled for Duke to go inside, to find supplies, to call an ambulance. My back door slammed and Stephen scuddled across the lawn to his car. The bullet had pushed straight through Holt's shoulder. His blood found its way to the air beneath my fingers.

"My boy is not dead," he said. "My boy, he's alive."

"He's alive, Holt," I promised him. "I'm alive."

Duke brought out gauze, a syringe, and the local anesthetic I'd asked for. I did my best to make sure Holt was comfortable as we waited for the paramedics to arrive. I was awestruck, my heart echoing in my chest as I looked down at the old man's pained but placid features. I was amazed to see myself in him, wondering why I had not noticed before. I wanted to see myself in him, to see myself looking back. The curvature of my nose. My jawline. Thin lips. The ambulance arrived.

"He's over here!"

The men rushed the gurney passed me, kneeling next to Maybelle. The woman who could be my mother lay in a broken pile on the grass, her limbs akimbo. I hadn't even noticed her go down. I had been so focused on the shot. On Holt's wound.

"She's unresponsive."

"Bag her."

Another team arrived to tend to Holt. A woman's soft hands pushed under mine to take over in applying pressure to his shoulder. They moved swiftly, efficiently loading the two into the ambulances. I stood silently, the blood drying and scabbing on my palms.

Maybelle had not been struck. Her autopsy revealed an aneurysm, a tiny clot of blood cells pushing through her veins to lodge within the frontal lobe.

"That's what did it," Squalls told me.

The two of us were on Maybelle's island, sorting through the belongings strewn about her little shack. We were trying to make sense of what to do with the tools of her calling, the MacBethian ephemera she'd left behind. Without saying it, I could tell Squalls expected me to step into her shoes, the animal doctor finding pure nature within what his estranged mother had bequeathed him.

"If that hadn't done it though," he told me, "the cancer would've. They told me her colon, her kidneys, they were eaten through with black."

He hadn't said a word about Holt. He didn't need to. Both of us knew where he was, how he was coping. He'd survived the bullet fired from Duke's gun. He'd survived the trial in Albany. He'd been sent up the Milledgeville, to the State Asylum there, where everyday he told the doctors that Colt was not with him anymore, that the gun had shot him right out through the shoulder. Like the swamp had sucked the duality of the old man's mind right from him. He wrote me letters through the coming years. I never wrote back.

Squalls stood with his fists tapping his hips as he stared through Maybelle's doorway.

"What do you think we ought to do with the sow and her piglets?" he asked me.

I looked out to the rutting pigs, watching the young ones

snort and chase the chickens across the dewy undergrowth. They seemed so innocent, so unprepared for what the swamp had in store for them.

Colt's eyes watched me from the trees. I could feel him, waiting there on the pathway back to the airboat, not yet wiling to relinquish the murky tangle of the peat moss filtering through the waters. I knew he was waiting for me, waiting to take me home.

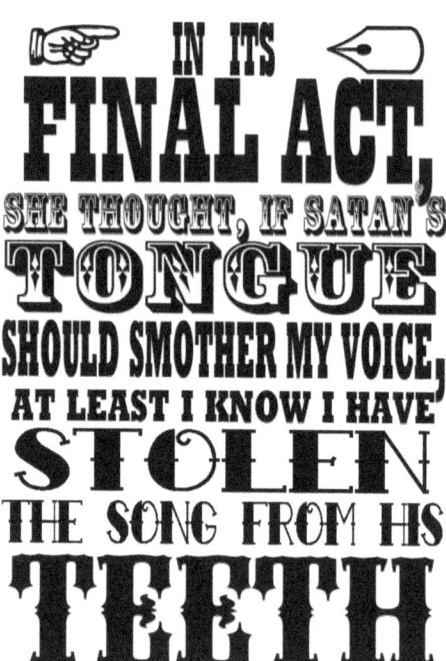

IN ITS FINAL ACT, SHE THOUGHT, IF SATAN'S TONGUE SHOULD SMOTHER MY VOICE, AT LEAST I KNOW I HAVE STOLEN THE SONG FROM HIS TEETH

WE
TREMBLE
AS WE
SINK

IF ANYONE HEARS MY VOICE

Marjorie Tilner's skirt strained at the seams of the beige fabric. She had her right leg pulled up, as much as the knee-length pencil skirt would allow, and pressed hard against the smallish dresser in her bedroom, her black high heel slipping free as she rocked the ball of her foot for leverage. Both her arms were raised, the left one pulling down as the right pushed upward until--

The bobby pin slid into place, locking in the same instant that Marjorie finished the count in her head. Forty-two pins circled her crown, pulling her hair up at the root while fixing the straw hat that, as she saw it, perfectly completed the jacketed ensemble she had donned in order to send her praises up to God. The mirror atop her dresser reflected the sweating brow of Jesus, peering upward in agony. Although born and raised a Baptist, Marjorie had always liked the Catholic iconography and had chosen a particularly heartfelt rendition of Christ's crucifixion to hang above her bed. The sweat and blood trickling down from His crown of thorns had always served to remind her of the real struggles one could face. She pulled a tissue from its box and dabbed at her forehead, careful to avoid smudging her mascara onto her pale foundation. She pursed her lips, checking for the fourteenth time the fluidity of the markings left by her lip liner.

"Do you not know that your body is a temple," she said, wiping a bit of smudged lipstick from the corner of her mouth. "Therefore honor God with your body." She added the "First Corinthians Six" impulsively, like a spelling bee champion repeating the word at the end of the round.

There's a fine line between painting a pleasing portrait for the Lord and looking like a gussied up trollop—Marjorie's mother had told her so many years back—and many years back Marjorie had come close to crossing that line herself. Now though, she had the subtleness necessary to stave off the hellfires down pat. She wore only a trace amount of pale blue, almost gray, eye shadow now, and always that color since Pastor Latwell had complimented the shade. Her lips, too, were always rubbed with a coral tone because Latwell had once told her it "looked nice." Pastor Latwell was the most righteous man Marjorie had ever known. He understood what pleased God. Marjorie knew she was right to listen to Latwell if she wanted to get into Heaven. He could show her the path.

A noise from outside pulled Marjorie's head from the clouds, and she hurried out to the black sedan idling in her driveway, smiling at Regina Johnson who was sitting in the driver's seat, and pulling her front door to without bothering to lock it. Marjorie and Regina had been friends since grade school and had sat together in the third row orchestra side pew since their mothers had let them sit away from the family during the sermon. It was comforting to both of them, almost part of the ritual of worship.

"I'm sorry, Betha," Marjorie called out as she neared the car and noticed the woman propped up in the passenger seat. "I need to ride in the front. I get car sick if I'm sitting in the back, and besides which there is not nearly enough room back there for my hat."

Marjorie stopped to preen for a moment so both women could take in the ensemble she'd put together. Betha pulled herself out of the vehicle to switch seats, barely even looking at Marjorie as she began to twist her girth towards the door. She seemed to lose her breath as she pushed at the handle to get the door open, and Marjorie wondered what it was that made Regina such a bleeding heart when it came to Betha Randolph. Betha wasn't much of a talker. She obviously had no sense of self-control when it came to the steakhouse buffet. She wore tennis shoes, most times, or even sometimes slippers into the House of the Lord. And her husband was a no good lay-about. The rumors clothes-lining around town about him were enough to make Satan himself go a deeper shade of red.

Marjorie tapped her foot against the dusty gravel of her driveway, still waiting for Betha to get herself up and out of her seat. She sighed audibly, checking the gold watch at her wrist before crossing her arms.

"We don't have all day, Betha. If Pastor Latwell has already started in on his sermon..."

"Oh, hush now, Marjie," Regina playfully scolded from behind the wheel. "We've got plenty of time."

Betha stepped to open the rear door as Marjorie slid gracefully into the front passenger seat, sliding the seat back to give herself room to stretch her legs forward a bit. Betha stared at the space remaining in the back for a moment before trying to push her way in.

"Be a dear, Betha, and don't push so much on my seat while you're entering Regina's vehicle. You'll cause sags in the upholstery. And be sure not to crinkle the brim of my new hat. My new hat which, might I say, was quite pricey, and that I'm surprised neither one of you ladies has commented on, Regina."

"It's a lovely hat. I was there when you bought it."

"I know that, but this is the first time you've seen it on me with the full outfit. It makes quite the difference. Lets the Lord know I consider His house with enough respect and dignity not to stroll in wearing sweat pants from the Dollar Depot. You all in, Betha? Make sure you pull the door closed tight."

As they drove, Marjorie tried to keep her head as straight as possible. She was angled with her back slightly toward her door, leaning forward in the direction of the steering wheel so as to give the brim of her hat enough breadth. She kept her eyes trained forward on Regina's hands clasping the wheel at ten and two so she wouldn't have to see Betha's peach excuse-for-a-dress that clung to her body disproportionately, or the smug look in Regina's eye each time her new half carat engagement ring glinted in the Sunday morning sunlight.

"Betha, on Tuesday Marjie and I are meeting with a caterer who's coming over from Valdosta to sample cakes. You want to join us?"

"Of course she does."

Marjorie spoke for Betha, attempting to clip the conversation on the upcoming nuptials as short as possible. Maid of Honor or not, she just could not summon the excitement she felt she should have for the occasion. Perhaps it was the strain the bobby pins were placing on her hairline. She could feel the tension rising at her temples and rubbed there to force it to subside. Or was it that Regina's ring was just as garish and disproportionate as Betha's clothes? The way the ring tilted toward first one side and then the other, to rest on her pinky for a moment and then shift its girth to her middle finger and then back again, never resting, a pendulum clicking back and forth, counting the days down, in Marjorie's eyes was not all that different from the swishing of synthetic fabric Betha was wrapped with in the sedan's rear bench seat. Her garments always clung more to her backside than her hips, more to her stomach than her breasts, leaving wispy, unfulfilled swatches around her shoulders with nothing better to do than sag and wrinkle, shifting in formation with Betha's every breath or spasm. Betha's clothes and now Regina's ring reminded Marjorie of all the false beauty in the world. They showed Marjorie just how the Devil himself was creeping into reality everyday, even now, even in her own life, shifting the grandeur of God's great creations only slightly, just enough to get a toe in the door. Enough pushes in and Satan could appear, could capture a heart wholly with no one ever the wiser. If Marjorie was not careful, he would take Regina right out from under her.

"Can you believe it?" Regina was saying. "In less than four weeks I'll be Mrs. Patrick Drake!"

"It---"

"It will be a beautiful wedding," Marjorie spoke up, raising her voice above what must have been the seat straining beneath Betha mixed with the exasperated sigh of the pressure Betha's girth placed on her lungs. "Your world is finally becoming right in the eyes of the Lord."

"Speaking of being in His eyes, Marjie. Pat wants to start sitting with us during the sermons. He thinks... We think it's appropriate to do so before the actual wedding, to let Jesus know we're serious about this union. He's giving us this last week as a sort of Church bachelorette party, and then next week will join us."

"How lovely."

"You're not upset by this, are you, Marjie? He is going to be my husband, you know."

"Why ever would I be upset by this?" Marjorie's voiced flittered an octave higher than usual. "You always seem to be bringing new folks into the fold with us. It's just an honor to be there with them as they receive the glory of our God."

Pastor Latwell perched at the top of the cement steps leading into the sanctuary of the church. He grasped his Bible firmly in his left hand, touching it gently with his right before and after each extension out to shake the hands of his congregation. His smile seemed warm and genuine. His hair was perfectly combed, barely giving away the thinning spot at his crown.

"Greetings, Miss Tilner, Miss Johnson," Pastor Latwell welcomed the women as they ascended the steps. "Mrs. Randolph, it is a pleasure to have you join us this fine Sunday. Will your husband be gracing us today?"

"Doubtful," Marjorie scoffed, taking Pastor Latwell's hand into her own. "We are just so pleased to be here to hear you impart the Word unto us."

The pastor squeezed Marjorie's hand for what she perceived to be a few seconds longer than he spent with the others in the congregation. His eyes warmed her palms, and she worried her countenance would betray her. She could feel the onslaught of her mortal sin coursing through her body, in the moments of the handshake threatening to take over. She smiled at her resilience in ending the grasp.

As they neared the front of the sanctuary, Marjorie stopped cold. She gripped tightly at Regina's arm. Betha stood awkwardly behind them, shifting her weight from foot to foot and if uncomfortable standing before the wooden crucifix nailed above the pulpit.

"It's okay, Marjie," Regina assured her. "We'll just take the pew behind them."

Marjorie's body seemed to her to be moving on autopilot as she slid onto the red fabric cushion of the oak bench. Her eyes stayed trained on the family that sat before them. The drops of sweat on the man's neck appalled her, how they pooled there and soaked into the collar of his white button-up. The woman's gold hoop earrings dangled all-together too low, threatening each time she moved her head to catch onto the shoulder pads of her navy blue skirt suit. And the children: two of them, jostling around in their seats, kicking their feet against the hymnals that adorned to back of the pew in front of them, no doubt irritating the tranquility of the deacons sat there, the men too attuned with the light of the Lord to say anything to the hoodlums interrupting their sanctity.

"That is our pew," Marjorie insisted, assuring the emphasis she placed on "our" did not go unnoticed by Betha. "We have worshipped from that position for now on twelve years."

"Oh, come now, Marjie. They are new here. We should be neighborly and not make a fuss."

"All the more reason to let them know. We don't want to lose our seats entirely to these late-to-worshippers." She turned pointedly to Betha. "If we'd arrived just a bit earlier, I imagine that all of this could have been avoided."

The congregation rose to their feet to begin the service with a staid rendition of "How Great Thou Art." As the song progressed, Marjorie leaned forward to place her lips near the woman's ear. Marjorie was pretty sure she was the matriarch of the family, standing there gurgling what she probably thought was a soulful rendition of God's hymn, but that Marjorie viewed simply as forced and show-y. She could smell the woman's skin cream, surprised at how quickly it filled the air around her. She'd been around black people before—as a child in school, or even now at the grocery store—but she'd never felt the air around her so fully immersed in the scent of their hair, of their skin. It was making her dizzy.

She wanted to tell the woman that she was in her seat, as a courtesy for next time, should they come back to the church. She needed to tell her that, but the fragrance was intoxicating. She tightened her jaw, wondering how to rectify raising her voice to God with not breathing. She recoiled from the smell, but it seemed to follow her back into her own pew. It was filling the holy air of the church, its earthly aroma ripening. The congregation around her, the choir behind the pulpit, no one noticed her pain. The persistent morning sun beamed through the high, colored panes of glass as if unaware of the darkness overtaking the sanctified ground. Marjorie was overwhelmed. Her eyes watered, and her vision became obscured by the demons writhing with the hum of the hymn.

The light struck the diamond on Regina's left hand, blinding Marjorie even after she closed her eyes in an attempt to regain composure. Her temples strained at the pull of her hat. She breathed deeply and again the sweet scent of tea tree oil and coconut filled her nostrils. Her knees weakened. The forty-two pins circling her consciousness like a crown of thorns ripped her hair at the root, clawed her skin in tiny, unceremonious gestures. She no longer felt safe. Insects hissed at her from the walls. Snakes crawled through the aisles, nesting beside the spare Bibles and Hymnals the church provided alongside the back of the oak pews.

"Marjorie doesn't look good, Regina."

Betha's overt drawl pounded at Marjorie's temples. Her knees buckled beneath her, and she fell backwards onto the cushion of the pew. As she landed, her head snapped backwards. The nape of her neck collided with the rounded curve of the pew-back. She felt the straw brim of her hat crush as she slid down, jostling the pins she'd so carefully placed and sending an agonizing fire through her body as they wrenched loose and sprung upwards into the dimming, putrid air.

She heard a communal gasp. The angels looking on from the apex of the sanctuary shielded their eyes in horror, unable to descend into the hellish force that took over the congregation, that surrounded Marjorie, centered in on her. She willed stigmata; even though she was not Catholic, she wanted some sign to show her purity, to fight back the beasts of darkness intent on devouring her. Her thoughts cried out to Jesus, cried out her piety, her belief, her righteousness. She prayed to the Savoir.

Pastor Latwell appeared above her. His radiant light fought off the darkness that was encroaching on them, and he gently removed the remaining pins from Marjorie's hair and placed her hat gently aside. He leaned toward her trembling face and put his lips on hers. She closed her eyes and he breathed his life into her, imbuing her lungs with the light and grace that only the Almighty could give. The warmth spread through her body, filled her heart and pushed electricity through her limbs, resuscitating her. His breath moved in and out of her, merged with hers. Pastor Latwell gave her direct access to the Holy Spirit. It moved through her, made her want to speak in tongues.

Marjorie's arms flew upward, wrapping around Pastor Latwell's shoulders, pulling his head closer to hers. Together they could fight off the darkness and the demons that were overwhelming their sanctuary. Together they could bring the Word of God back into the world. She felt him writhe above her. It made her want him more. She held his lips to hers, willing to be consumed. The din of the congregation began to burrow back through her consciousness. She heard the gasps, the revolt of those who could not understand the glory unfolding before them.

Pastor Latwell's palms found her shoulders, massaging them. She heard a deep rumble coming from his chest, a muffled assurance as his tongue attempted to work within the passion of their kiss. He seemed to be pushing away from her. He wanted to cry out his love. But Marjorie wasn't ready yet to let go. She needed this. Needed his light. His breath was coming sharper now, betraying the even pace he had begun with. His tongue darted wildly as he attempted the guttural syllables of desire.

"Marjie," Regina's voice sounded loudly to her right. "You fainted, dear. You stopped breathing. Doctor Johnson, the new guest in our congregation, is giving you mouth to mouth. You need to let him go."

Marjorie opened her eyes. She stared upwards into the face of the Devil. His black skin beaded with sweat; his eyes filled with terror and vileness and locked on hers. Marjorie bit down hard on his tongue. She gagged as her mouth filled with his blood. The blood of Lucifer. Her teeth began to grind against themselves. She had severed the serpent's forked tongue. No longer could he lure women with his deceptions to dance nude under the light of the moon. No longer could he persuade sin from the fruits of God's Knowledge. She choked on the blood, on the slimy dance of the Devil's flesh. In its final act, she thought, if Satan's tongue should smother my voice, at least I know I have stolen the song from his teeth.

The angels huddled at the apex of the sanctuary opened their wings. They brought forward their trumpets. Marjorie knew they were welcoming her into the light that began to fill her vision. She knew she would soon be home. Marjorie saw a new Heaven and a new Earth for the first Earth and Heaven had passed away.

NOTHING NEW

When I was three and she was five, Sissy's red patent mary janes used to bruise my shins beneath the table and get stuck in the mud along the driveway, in the patches where the gravel had washed away after every time it rained. When I was five, those shoes sat in my closet and my mama yelled at me for never wearing them, saying how they were perfectly good and beggars cain't be choosers and waste not want not and all those other altruisms parents use to explain the world, and my shins would ache every time I opened the slatted doors of my closet and looked down at those red shoes with the little brass buckle heaped up with last night's pajamas and yesterday's under-roos.

When I was seven and Sissy was eight and three quarters she took my plastic Jack-o-Lantern before we got back to our driveway and dumped all the candy out and took all the Mars Bars for herself and left me with the SweeTarts and apples. But I only got them after she had taken a piece to make sure they weren't poisoned and a bite to search for razor-blades because that's what she'd heard old scary people do on Halloween when they can't get their jollies any way other than by hurting little girls. I asked her what "getting their jollies" meant and she told me I would learn once I got to her grade at public school, and I told her I wanted to know now because by then she would know all this other stuff and getting their jollies would be old news and she wouldn't want to talk about it with me and she bit into an apple and blood started coming out of her mouth and I screamed and ran and she started laughing and spitting out a blood capsule.

When I was ten and Sissy was twelve I heard Mama say "Priscilla and Susan are coming with me" in that order because Sissy's name always came first, and then I heard Daddy say "Like hell you're taking my daughter" in the singular like that because I'd heard him swear before that he was in the Gulf around the time I should have been conceived and I pictured him kicking back with one of his Daddy's Juice Cans in Panama City and Sissy told me that the sand in my imagination was right but I was a couple million miles off on the location. Then she shushed me and Daddy didn't even look at me when he came to tuck me in that night and Sissy spent a long time staring at the wall and Mama's headlights never once turned back up the driveway.

When Sissy was fifteen and I was thirteen, I got all her old training bras and tried them on and they may as well have been mud flaps for nonexistent tires the way they just sat there doing nothing but making everybody laugh at the promise of a hot chick silhouette. Plus when I was thirteen and Sissy was fifteen she lost the key to her diary and I found it and I hid it and she started leaving it unlocked. I read through the pages, trying to feel everything that she was feeling and exactly what high school would be like. I kissed all the boys she grew tired of and once I even borrowed her old, grass-stained cheerleading uniform and wore it to seduce this boy she'd written about in her diary and he just laughed at me because of the yellow and puke green stains. When I made it to high school he called me "Skidmark" in the hallway.

When I was sixteen and Sissy was eighteen she got herself pregnant and Daddy called her swamp trash even though he was born here too and his whole family was still spread around the different areas of the marsh. Sissy swore she was a virgin and Daddy said that some chick had already used up that line a couple thousand years ago. He batted her ear and she cried and that was the first time Daddy ever lifted a hand to anyone as far as I can remember so Sissy had that first too. I found her cigarettes and I smoked and Sissy found me out back and lit one up and sat down beside me and didn't yell at me for stealing. I told her that smoking was bad for the baby and he'd have webbed feet and a lizard tail and she looked at me and her mascara was all smudged and welling up around her eyes and I think it was the exact same color–Midnight Sea or something like that, black with a hint of blue—that Mama used to wear before she left first Sissy and then me and I felt that same sympathy for her she must've felt for me all those years back when she shushed me and tried to show me Saudi Arabia on a map.

Daddy didn't talk to Sissy for a month except to mumble stuff about how he couldn't understand why the Norfolk women—which was Mama's maiden name—expected the Madisons—which was our last name—to believe in the miracle of miraculous conception. Sissy and I would sit out back and suck down nicotine as Daddy would rampage around the house and we would stare at the cypress trees and not talk, or watch the swamp gas spark through the thickets of honeysuckle and kudzu and pretend sometimes—or at least I did after Sissy told me she did—that the flashes of burning were Mama's headlights sending out some Morse Code what-to-do. I told Sissy it'd probably be more clichés and she just took a long drag off her cigarette and I took a long drag off of mine and I asked her whose it was and she was quiet for a long time before she turned to me and said "Roger." I said "Roger Bogle" and she said "Yeah" and I flicked the cherry off my cigarette and went inside smiling 'cause I'd had Roger Bogle last year and she was barely two months along.

Andrew Forrest Baker

WE
TREMBLE
AS WE
SINK

HOLLOW
BONES

Her hair grew in curly, and then her eyes crossed, but that was probably from trying to pinpoint a center in her lopsided nose, so I guess you could say, she was doomed to be a little off-center right from the beginning. She took cabs on a wild goose chase for her house, directing them to turn here and then there, heading in circles around town, but only because when she rode her bike that was the way she knew to get home. And maybe also a bit because it was one of the only times she felt in control of the situation, one of the few moments she believed she was powerful. That's why she'd become a teacher, so she could feel as if she were in command of some part of her life, but her students—third graders, all of them—mocked her lazy eye and humped nose on the monkey bars when they thought they were out of earshot, but weren't.

The man she'd met at the VFW was a Shriner and a zealot and a veteran of the first Gulf War, but, as far as he flattened view of him could tell, was cute enough and wasn't too much older and seemed to genuinely like her except for when his fingers got tangled up in her hair. He proposed to her on the third date and her mom had said, "what's a little PTSD amongst dowries," so she'd agreed to a small ceremony on her uncle's property in late October. He'd seen to it that a patch of cotton was left untouched, its brown and twiney stems giving way to radiant but slightly off explosions of white that hid the coloring on her hand-me-down dress. She'd agreed to the wedding and agreed with the vows but she hadn't agreed to a photographer so when the man was called back to action and disappeared–captured or killed or AWOL–somewhere in the caves of Afghanistan, she had no way of remembering what he looked like when he smiled directly at her. She'd said "no" to the photographs because, with the way her eyes fell, she had trouble with depth perception, and the heinousness of looking at a two-dimensional depiction when that was all she could perceive of real life anyway could quite possibly drive her mad.

She took to wearing black, as a widow should, and raising cats, like the spinsters in her favorite novels, and also bird watching as if the dampened color scheme and feline instincts around her had co-mingled into a new persona. At first she simply believed that she longed for their freedom–a mundane reasoning, she was forced to confess, that made her long to look deeper into her enthrallment. That their hollow bones were akin to her aching heart seemed too much the stuff of the romantics and only reminded her further of being grounded, a devastation when the ground served only in effigy of him. Too, their coloring, verbose and flashy for the males and camouflaged for the females, harkened to how she would sometimes picture them together, even when he was in his desert tans and boarding the bus to the base. And if it all just reminded her of her mother's feathered hair, then that didn't seem to be enough either.

Her lessons at school soon turned to the fowl, using the birds to teach the children syntax and tenses–"When the robin redbreast fly/flied/flew across her doorway, Mrs. Childress know/knew/knowed she would soon have company."–and cursive–"The lowercase 's' should swoop up and around like the great wing of the heron taking flight."–and the children began to doodle pictures that accentuated her beak of a nose and hazed, glass-like eye. She would find them inside of the desks' pencil drawers and even once etched into the wood by Tommy Nickels. She confiscated notes in which her garments feathered out around her shoulders, and eventually took solace in knowing that her students were able to, at the very least, render a fine parody of a crow.

Still the birds in the thicket behind her house excited her, and on birthdays she would find small wooden whistles, hand carved by the principal and left in the teacher's lounge, meant to emulate their noises and draw them closer. She would never use the birdcalls though, thinking them an affront to the creatures' true nature, to their freedom and their flighty ways.

The principal was a squat man, with a protruding mandible and tiny, beady eyes. She pictured him in flattened, flitting motions, his pocket knife working over chunks of balsa wood as his lip twitched with each swipe of the blade. She'd noticed the tic in the hallways at school, as he stood outside of his office and she took advantage of the water fountain. It wasn't constant, but in her mind it defined his fleshy lips against the stark, sharp beaks of her birds, catching in snarling motions amidst the wiry bristles of his beard, as if he wanted more than anything to talk, but could not. She pitied him, as she was sure people pitied her, but found herself touched by his gestures, keeping the birdcalls alongside the cards he'd made—each wishing her a joyous date of birth and documenting both the common and scientific names of the birds the whistles were meant to summon—on display throughout her house.

She petitioned the school board and sent permission slips home with the students for a trip to the State Park to hear about the wildlife. She'd asked the new guy there—an older fellow, but just out of veterinary school, with kind eyes and long limbs who'd just moved up from Florida—to focus on the fowl in hopes that the kids would garner at least a bit of the affections she felt for her feathered fascinations. She needed another adult to supervise the field trip and the principal volunteered, riding silently beside her in the front seat of the school bus, lip twitching and eyes trained on the back of the driver's balding head. The students fidgeted in their seats, or threw wads of paper and spitballs at their classmates, or snuck the desserts out of the brown bag lunches she'd asked the parents to pack. Two miles seemed like two hundred, or at least they did to her, wishing that she could travel as the crow flies, to make her rainy cab rides home more manageable, to free herself of the twitching chaos that surrounded her.

The bus pulled to a stop and the kids piled out, spouting off the numbers she'd assigned them when they left the classroom, with only a few of them out of order as new alliances had formed during the ride over and the children had grouped up for the outing. They seemed as excited as she was. She smiled and ignored the likelihood that they were simply encouraged by the lack of desks and cinder block walls and imagined instead that they were driven by the coming knowledge of their world. The swamp had a way of invigorating people—locals and tourists alike—and the closer you got to the heart of it, the more you could feel the creatures writhing within your own veins. They rippled through her, turning her blood warm and cold in alternating pulses that mimicked the tenses of an evolution stuck–regressing and progressing in an equal pull of the present.

The swamp vet approached them smiling, a hawk perched upon his leather glove and gauntlet. She fell in love immediately: the length of the majestic neck, stiff and skyward, twitching only slightly as the head cocked to asses the onlookers and betraying only a slight ruffle of feathers, was captivating. The principal herded the class into a tight group away from the majestic claws that she knew could strike suddenly and from any distance within the hawk's sightline. After a quick welcome, they ventured inside of the faux-log encampment set up there by the state and took their seats before a wall of cages containing their lessons on the wild, or at the most, the teachings on the aspects which had been tamed and documented and numbered. The girls squealed at the snakes, but reached out to touch their scaly musculature even before some of the boys. They all rejoiced, students and teacher, everyone except the principal, when the swamp vet released a small mouse for the hawk to slay. The claws wrapped around the furry brown body, keeping it alive, through possibly in shock, as the hawk rose to the rafters and only then punctured a lung with a black talon. The principal's shriek sounded so close to that of the rodent that at first she wasn't sure he'd even made a sound. The kids were sure though, and mocked him on the bus ride back to the elementary school.

She amassed seven birdcalls, spent seven birthdays a widow, before he had the courage to speak directly to her. He was huddled in the corner of the teacher's lounge, surrounded by a rat's nest of ripped paper and twine and scotch tape, as he desperately attempted to wrap his latest gift—a blue-winged teal call—when she entered and caught him off-guard. He stood and presented the call to her in his cupped hands, his stubby fingers nicked from the blade of his pocketknife. He tried to say "happy birthday," or at least that's what he intended, but it came out instead as "would you like to eat dinner sometime?" He blushed, and she heard the implied "with me," and accepted before she realized it, deciding so out of pity, she thought, and not a genuine interest in the bulbous, rodent-like man before her.

Storm clouds had spent the week leap-frogging through the atmosphere, challenging the swamp with a seething moisture to see who would reign in the area—the land or the sky—before finally giving in and conceding their liquid to the earth just as school let out. She moved her bicycle into her classroom, wiped the moisture from its vinyl seat and its chain, then made her way to the administrative center to call a cab. The principal emerged from his office and, more gallant now, offered her a ride home through the downfall.

They rode mostly in silence, save for when she directed him right or left, and he let her stay cool and dry in the air conditioned car when the tire struck a broken pine branch strewn across the road and thudded with each rotation of the axel, tripping along in a descending volume and frequency like a bird's wings landing to a full stop. He put on the spare tire lodged beneath the floorboard of his trunk, and drove slowly, for her safety, as the donut attempted to find its grip on the rain-soaked roadways. Even though he lived in the opposite direction. Even though he was dripping water like a wet rat and his upper lip was more shivering now than tic-ing. When they pulled into her driveway she felt it only right to incite him inside so he could dry off and not catch his death of cold before their first date.

She fluttered up the steps as he trudged along behind her, then stood dripping on the linoleum floor as she went in search of a clean towel. While he busied himself with the cloth, drying first his face and hair, then patting down his suit and kicking the towel through the puddle he'd left on the floor, she searched through her kitchen cupboards. Any southern woman worth her salt was required to offer up some form of nourishment to her guests, expected or un-invited, and she'd be damned if this occasion would tarnish what there was of her reputation. She managed to pull together a platter of mixed nuts and sunflower seeds, a few vanilla wafer cookies, and some wrapped cold cuts, and placed them in the center of her table. She poured glasses of sweet tea and he joined her in the room, the towel extended before him like an offering he wasn't sure he should give. She laid it flat to dry across her sink, and invited him to join her for a spell, her cadence so similar to the way she remembered her mother's that it startled her.

He took a sip of the tea and helped himself to some of the bo-logna and ham she'd wrapped with slices of American cheese. She pecked at the unsalted peanuts and stared just past him to a stain on the wall above her stove. Neither of them spoke as the minutes ticked by them, echoing the gentle sputter of water as the storm be-gan to break outside. The ice rattled against his face as he took a final swig from his glass and tried to subtly use the sleeve of his jacket to wipe the moisture from his beard. She rose and reached out her arm to grab his cup to refill it. His hand covered hers and they froze there, finally looking at one another. His fat though flattened figure seemed to come to life in her eye—rounded out in a startling three dimensions that urged touch, like the mouse they'd seen those months back begging for the talon of the hawk. She felt like she could devour him.

It's been so long since she'd known a man's touch, after all, since she'd felt anyone so near to her. And he liked her too, she could tell. The hunger was there, overtaking his small eyes. They were nearly black, she thought, pupils dilated with desire.

They moved swiftly. He pushed her platter aside and laid her down on the table, a bird on her back. Her want of control vanished, dissipating with the storm. His lips met her cheek. She bristled beneath the sharpness of the hair circling his mouth like whiskers, like fur. He kissed down her neck to her breast, wetting the black fabric there as she arched her back to reach the zipper behind her, making him want her all the more. She pushed her garment to her waist, and his mouth found her stomach. He relished in its tenderness. The prick of his beard sent shockwaves through her body.

She felt his teeth move across her skin. His tongue lapped at her. Her head tilted back. He moved his mouth into her, through her. She was exposed, flapping her arms for a grounded flight that encouraged him further in. Her helplessness was intoxicating. He needed her as much as he was sure she needed him. He longed to be inside her, to crawl beneath her hollowed out ribcage, to root around in her viscera, to ground her there with him, to find what she tasted like inside. He wanted to see what made her who she was, why it was that despite all her troubles, her curly hair and crooked nose and lazy eye, she seemed to be able to soar, to be the freest among them all. He was compelled to get inside her, to discover how she could fly. His teeth found passage first, at her most tender spot, followed by his whiskers and his tongue, his stubby claws and his beady eyes.

The swamp grew quiet outside, using dusk as an excuse to listen in on her swan song, to welcome them both into the night.

'Cross the line, there's white. It's in the sand. In the seashells. They say it's blinding, but I'm willing to wager it's not nearly as blinding as it gets over here in the pitch of night, when the smells of the still waters come gurgling up my nostrils and the cicadas and the owls and the night crawlers all start their songs and not even the lightning bugs or foxfires would dare to disturb the deprivation through the overload.

'Cross the line, there's laughter. We got laughter here too, but I mean, it's of a different sort. Our laughter is what gets us through the day, gets me through the monotony, gets me through the bogs. But their laughter—they got Disney and beaches; we got sand traps and the Pig'an. They got Mai Tais and six-toed tabby cats and Panama Jack; and we got rotgut and that's about it lessen we want to suck down the swill from the swamp. Makes no difference either way after a while. The St. Mary's is clean enough. Ships used to admire her for her depth and her purity, but after seeing Old Man Richards relieving his willy into her I ain't getting my lips nowhere close.

You grow up here and you're a man at twelve years. You got to be. I had to be. Elsewise you ain't got much of a chance in your daily navigations of the land. Mostly that's 'cause there ain't much land to be had so you've got to be all the more careful. Or else that's a lie we tell to the folks from across the line so they don't venture in. Truth is, you do have to grow up early, but there's plenty of land amidst the waters. We just don't want no jealousy of all we got. The snake berries that ain't poison if you pick 'em right and taste sweeter than the oranges from across the line. The treasures of the Indian Mounds that the government tells us have got to stay right where they are on account of their historicness. The thunder of a footfall that, if placed just right, can bring down a forest. We got the swamp, so we get to be gods.

'Cross the line they got bobble-headed bottle-blonds in bikinis, gallivanting around the surf on their knock-kneed stems with their bare mid-drifts sparkling with acrylic stones shaped like the Playboy Bunny or an Aztec sun or a teardrop. They got tanned boys with dangly arms and over-active oil glands all piling out of half-off bar nights without a single spec of soil saddled up under their fingernails, their crotch rockets lipsticking up out of their drawstring board shorts like a coon-hound every time a bitch in heat sashays by. This side we got calloused palms and corned feet and tan lines where they're supposed to be. I got Betha at home with her lopsided, beefsteak ankles and her pork-n-bean thighs fighting with all their might to cover up her kneecaps; and I got Tess who's younger and thinner with her knowledge of a razor and her molasses cunt that I see sometimes on the side.

This side you can get bitter real quick. I've seen it happen. Those weekend wonders and those white coats and those witch womyn (with the "y" like that, you know), they can all talk a big game about the Okefenokee being a place of purification and how the peat moss filters the water and cleans it pure before it goes out to the Gulf or out to the At-lantic. But those folks are just here for a day or two. The rest of us who's here all the while know that all that mush the moss filters out has got to go somewhere, and if you ain't careful it's going to go right up into you. It's nothing per-sonal. It's nothing malevolent. That's just how it is. 'Cross the line they got the sand that gets stuck in places you didn't know were on your body until you felt that tiny module itch-ing its way up through your folds. This side we got all the left over sludge that the rest of the world ain't apt to handle.

'Cross the line they got little girls, and sometimes they come here and then they go home women. They come over or one of us brings them over and they bleed, spill their blood on Georgia's red clay versus their white sands, or if they used to ride horses they just let their eyes do the flushing, and then they walk back across and the swamp just cleans it all up. No harm done. And they get to be as grown up as they were acting in their bathing suits and see-through wraps. No harm done. And we get feel like we escaped for a night. And the swamp just trembles all around and washes it all up and packs it all down and then one of us, usually me, will take on all that smut and just sit back and wait for the next one. Or I'll go see Tess. Or as a last resort I'll go on home to Betha. And Betha'll ask me when we're gonna move over there—when we're going to get out of the trailer and the pit and find a place on the beach with the fresh-caught oysters—and she'll tell me the swamp is making my soul dark and it's coming through my eyeballs now; and I'll tell her it's just a few grains of trouble and not to worry none and I'll climb up into my side of the bed and turn my back on hers and my hands will dip into my Fruit-of-the-Looms and I'll finger all around my manhood as I think about the last girl who wandered over to my truck and the girl before that and then the ones who didn't wander but looked enough like they wanted to so that made it okay.

Andrew Forrest Baker

LIKE ANYONE WOULD

Everybody here responds to the will o' the wisp. It doesn't matter where we are, if we can even see it. We all snap. We all freeze. For the teens, all gangly and pockmarked, all dreaming their escapisms, they pose in the flash of the paparazzi bulbs. The liver-spotted, varicosed folks, even those withering away at the Regal Plains Retirement and Nursing Village, they all go rigid in their attempt to avoid the light at the end of the shaft. As if by pausing for that split second they can fool Death away for a little bit longer, make him think they'd already passed. Even the cocks that a few of the men pit together in the shed out back from Walker's place pause in their attacks, talons stuck mid-strike, unyielding as if the air was suddenly sucked straight out and replaced by molasses. We all feel it. Our time riddled with sporadic respite—mid-step, mid-sentence, mid-thrust for the lucky ones. So slight the outsiders passing through toward the coast or camping out at the Park probably wouldn't even notice it. But it's there. They might smell the shifting waft of sulfur, the waltz of rotten egg and menstruation lumberjacking around their nostrils, and then chalk it all up to The Great Outdoors and move on. But the will o' the wisp, it's still there.

About two years back—no, now it's been more than five—when it happened, when I figured it all out, I was twenty-seven. Like anyone would at that age, I was self-involved enough that everything I'm telling you, most of it, came to me second-hand or in retrospect while downing glasses of rotgut at the end of Grayson's clapboard bar counter. But that's how most stories happen. That's what I was learning, what I was supposed to be absorbing, when it happened. There's always a filter. That's not the moral so much as just how it is. Something you should keep in mind. A shot of the swill Neal Grayson was passing off as sour mash and a memory. A walk down Church Street and a glimpse at the old High School Gym. And on and on like that until the pieces start to make some semblance of sense, to form the narrative arc that Miss Muldoon in high school was so fond of warbling on about.

I was off Thursdays from the paper factory about a half hour out of town, and I took that time to do my laundry for the week over at Delandra Jackson's house. She had a screen run 'round her back porch and about two summers ago some black guys who turned out to be her sons visiting from their grandma's in Mobile, Alabama with bulging forearms and sweat-riddled foreheads wrestled a banged-up washer/dryer set they'd picked up at the Goodwill on up there, and since I didn't have access to one at my apartment building she let me come over and use it between ten and two. I'd be out there trying to fold my underwear and listening to Delandra whoop and holler at the soap opera actors or the defendants on the televised court cases. If I stood just to the right of the dryer, I could peer in through the window over her kitchen sink. From there it was a straight shot down to the living room and Delandra's vinyl sofa with the blue and green floral print and foam stuffing sticking out where a cat she used to have had clawed its way through the stiff plastic. I danced with her once at prom, fifteen years previous, back when nobody else would on account of everybody predicting her future in garbage maintenance, and she repaid me with suds and rinse cycles. It was funny how those kids would use that as a put down when a lot of our fathers proudly picked up trash for a living. 'Course if they could see her now—let go from the convenience store, jobless, and collecting cats—they'd more than likely hold their breath and smile and avert their eyes as quickly as they could.

Delandra had passed overweight a good three or four cases

of Moonpies ago. Her upper arms folded around her elbows so that whenever she bent her hand from the Lay's bag and toward her mouth I imagined a puppeteer at work in the recesses of her gut, shifting levers up and down to make the function work. The way her forearm just stuck out of her body's girth, a sprout spurting out of a severed branch. The way her jilted and carnivorous movement seemed to happen devoid of any muscular tension. I had to remind myself of her kindness in letting me use her laundry machines while my mouth tried to curl into laughter at the scene, at her "Go, Judy"s and "You tell 'em, Judge Alex"s and her "Oh, Alejandro"s. Her skin was a rich ebony that darkened slightly around her smile lines and at her temples; her grey lips always flecked with salt and the orange coating from the chips she seemed to have stockpiled. Delandra lived off a government disability check that she'd picked up when her Type-2 Diabetes rendered her inefficient as a checkout girl at the gas station, and her eating habits seemed part insurance of her check retention, part suicide attempt.

She rarely spoke to me directly. She'd just nod as I let myself into her screened in porch and started pushing through my loads of dirty coveralls and t-shirts. Every now and again she'd ask me to run down to the corner store, down to where she used to work, to pick up a few 2 Liters of Coca Cola or tell me she was running low on her fabric softener because it was the agreement that I'd keep those sorts of things, the laundry supplies, in stock for her in return for using her machines. Most of the time though, she minded her business and I tried to mind mine. Like anyone would.

It was looking as if I was bound to finish up my laundry early that Thursday when Delandra started wailing from her living room. I ignored her at first, concentrating on creasing my t-shirts the way my mother had taught me—the way my father had liked his creased—when I caught glimpse of her through the window. She rocked back and forth on the sofa, building up her momentum to get her girth up to her feet. As she shuffled toward the kitchen window, I kept my eyes down, catching from their corners the tufts of hair that had freed themselves from the waxed and set waves that had been procured at Sister Sasha's Salon probably over a month ago. I figured she was just on a mission for more potato chips when her fist started pounding on the glass between us. As her hands hit the pane, they seemed to forget that they were a part of time, even time as slowed down by the molasses-thick humidity of the Georgia South. The skin pressed against the glass turned grey-to-white-to-grey as her knocking spread its force into the window, the fat of her fingers billowing outward like ripples in the Stillwater as the gators poked their heads out from underneath.

"I'm almost done," I told her. "I'll be gone in a bit."

"Boy, it ain't but noon twenty," she called back. "That ain't why I's knockin'. Now get yore skinny white ass up in here."

Delandra's voice was a contradiction to itself, part high pitched, part deep and gruff. I imagined the high pitched part was her old voice, the one she'd grown up with, and that the low part was the result of the weight she'd packed on pushing her vocal chords to a muffled lilt. When she spoke it sounded as if two people were struggling around in her girth; God's way of reconciling the space she was taking up, or at the very least some half-formed twin she'd swallowed down in the womb.

I paused at the back door, unsure of what to do. Delandra had never invited me into the house before. She'd always resigned me to the porch. Even when I picked up Twinkies and Coca-Cola for her, she'd had me leave them atop the dryer or else pass them through the window to her grabby fingers. My own fingers were clutching the doorknob so tightly the whites of my knuckles were spreading along and starting to send pins into my palms. Delandra huffed for me to hurry it up and I let the doorknob twist in my grasp. The backdoor didn't open into the side of the kitchen like I'd thought it would, but instead I was facing down a hallway that ran parallel to it.

"Get yer skinny ass in here 'fore the segment's over."

I heard Delandra's thundering footsteps as I made my way down the hall, barely noting the rooms that fed off to my left. After that the hallway opened up on the right to the dining room that separated the kitchen from the living room and as I passed through the doorframe I saw Delandra back on her couch and shaking her head at the TV like it'd turned into a rabid dog or some pit of snakes, looking all shocked and dumbfounded and a little bit scared.

"Old Holt Martin's done got up and sent to the loony bin."

As I joined Delandra on the couch, scrunching my body in close to the armrest to allow some space, albeit not much, between us, I let my eyes twist toward the newscast still underway on the screen. We hadn't seen a real murder in town in over ten years, so the local station was giving the find a lot of attention. Sure, there had been bodies that turned up, mostly in the county and therefore not actually part of the city jurisdiction, but even the majority of those had been either left-unsolved-and-assumed- or discovered to be victims killed elsewhere and transported in by folks thinking the swamp waters would swallow them up.

"You missed the part where they said that Bog Witch died too. And that Holt Martin was most likely that new vet's real daddy," Delandra laughed. "Stupid white folks can't even keep track of they own childrens. I may not have my boys here, but at least I's know where they is."

I barely had a second to breathe in before Delandra's entire massive body sent the signal that our conversation was over. I mumbled an I'll-show-myself-out and started back down the hallway, more slowly this time, taking in her house. The doorway into the hall started a few feet to the right from where the hallway actually ended in a closed and latched door. I turned left, toward the back porch and my laundry. The next room down was the bathroom, long and surprisingly narrow, with the john up at the far end, a counter and a mirror and sink running along the wall to my left and a tub in between me and the toilet. The tub was rounded on three of its sides, wall-bound; and then the front and back of the tub, assuming tubs have a front and a back, had those metal bars old people use for pulling themselves up and out of the water or hospice care nurses imagine using for bracing when holding under the geezers who make their lives so miserable. She'd told me once before, now I don't even remember why, that her weight had stopped her periods a while back, so I didn't see any Tampax boxes in there, but there were about twenty bottles of White Rain aerosol hairspray on the counter. After that was what I figured to be Delandra's bedroom. Through the doorframe, the door itself painted a pale dirty yellow and left hanging slightly ajar like it was caught somewhere in a kind of purgatory between opening and closing, her unmade bed sported threadbare cotton sheets, the center of which—and by center I mean starting there and spreading out almost clear to each side of the Queen mattress—held a pond rippling of sweat stains that haloed out toward the empty candy wrappers and half-drunken Coke cans on the nightstand. She didn't seem to have an alarm clock from what I could see, and the little black ants that invaded every Georgia home this time of year were having a field day with the bounty they'd discovered, relaying the tiny bits of sugar back to the mound like at any moment they could wake up and the beauty of their dream vanish.

I finished folding up my jeans in silence and tapped out a goodbye on the window to an un-answering Delandra before dragging my bags back home and stacking the clean clothes on top of my own unmade bed to put away later. As I stacked them out I noticed two of my white tees had gotten a pinkish tint to them somehow, probably a red bandana or something got tossed in with the load, and I tossed them both aside to use as dish rags around the house since I sure as hell wasn't going to wear pink out in public. Not in this town anyway. Some of the boys who'd made it out to college would come back down from Athens or Milledgeville or wherever and they'd have on bright pink shirts with the collars popped up, but that sure as hell weren't me. That's what a liberal arts education will do to a soul, pour it into pink and make it forget how to use its hands.

The next week, I lost half my morning. The foxfires were exploding undetected, spurred on by the heat of the early morning sun. It was already a quarter passed ten when I slung the netted laundry bag up over my shoulder like a poor man's Santa Claus and fought through my front door. It always stuck in the summer, the wood expanding from the moisture in the air and catching against the frame. My screen door had a note taped to it from Delandra, asking me to pick up a few things from the corner store in a labored yet highly fashioned script. Her letters slanted to the left and the ends of them festooned out into rehearsed and wild territory. It was sweet to look at, and made the snack foods and sugar waters she'd requested seem almost fancy, as if they were divine offerings to some forgotten god.

When I finally made it to her house, Delandra had the back window open above the washer. Two grabby palms shot through and I handed the bounty to her. I smiled as I answered her greeting, and went to work filling the machine. She left the window open and labored back to her couch.

"Commercial break," she called out, and I lobbed my socks and drawers into a pile away from my blue jeans.

I pulled myself atop the dryer to wait out the first twenty-minute cycle. I could hear Delandra chomping down on the chocolate fudge cookies over the low din of her television, over the swishing of spinning water and detergent, over the clicking rapture of cicadas and Georgia Thumpers. Mouth full, she exclaimed: "It's back!"

She told me Elissa and Elizabeth had been having an affair with the same man and were close to finding out. She said his infidelity to both of them was atrocious, but only made him sexier. She wondered aloud what would happen when they found out about one another, and how the writers would handle that since both women were played by the same actress. Elissa had a red wig; Elizabeth was naturally blonde.

"What I think they's gone do," she said during a commercial break, "is have one of them honkey bitches kill the other'n. With the first one's gun or painkillers or something."

I rotated a load to the dryer and started a new one on the wash cycle.

Two o'clock came amidst a flurry of names and farcical relationships, and as I slung the bag of newly laundered clothing over my shoulder, Delandra said, "You know these stories are on every weekday, don't you?"

I worked the evening shift on Tuesday, so I headed over the Delandra's with all the dirty fabric I could scrape together. I figured she wanted me there, that she needed company, that she forgot how it was to actually interact with someone. She hadn't invited me back inside, but she was leaving the window open and telling me the tidbits of other people's lives she studied with a fevered fury for hours each day. And I could listen or not, sitting there on the washing machine, listening for the foxfires out back, trying to figure out where my days were going.

The will o' the wisp, some say, is really just gas rising up from decaying plant and animal matter in the swamps and then igniting in the oxygen rich air. Others go on about how it's alien signals, some form of extraterrestrial communication. And people will counter that with stories on the drug trade and the drugs lost to the depths of the trembling earth and how they get burnt out and give us all hallucinations. When I'm sitting propped up on Delandra's back porch, I think about how the will o' the wisp is our escape, our chance at freedom, our chance at seeing the real story if we could only break through those frozen moments.

I don't tell Delandra that though. She was always just too happy droning on about the characters on her TV screen. She told me about how the Baron hit Elissa over the head with a candlestick and she fell to the ground and her red wig came straight off her head. They weren't twins—Elissa and Elizabeth—but were actually the same person the whole time. But how now Elissa was in a coma, so Elizabeth was too, and how no one could really be sure which of the two personalities was real and which would emerge from the imposed slumber of the candlestick clobbering. Delandra was sad because Elizabeth was meant for the Baron and she was losing so much time she could have been with him on account of the coma. Delandra liked Elizabeth. She thought the Baron and her had a real true love.

"And real, true love," Delandra said, "is mighty hard to come by. 'Specially 'round these parts. You gotta grab onto it when you see it and try real hard not to let it slip past."

My times on Delandra's porch became the highlights of my week. I stretched single loads of laundry into four. I tuned out the grating voice excitedly reenacting soap operas from the living room. I focused all of my attention on the wisp. On how to overcome its imposed stasis.

"Remember I told you how Elissa is in a coma?" Delandra asked. "Well, Elizabeth is in there with her. Crazy bitch is fighting with herself in her own head. Like anyone can ever win a self-contained battle." She guffawed. "You white folks sure has some funny ideas sometimes."

The real story was happening in the downtime, inside the moments of inactive equilibrium. I wanted to find a way into it. I wanted to find out where we went when time flashed still, where all those milliseconds left us afterward. I figured if I slowed myself down enough, I would be immune to the wisp. I figured I could learn to hold my breath.

I'd stopped taking laundry over to Delandra's altogether, and she had pushed her TV around to where I could see it from the window. She sat at her dining room table now instead of on the couch, and jerked her head back and forth between me and the screen as she spoke, rubbernecking like northbound drivers when there's a wreck in the southbound lanes. I was just sitting there now, half-assed in my listening and really trying to solve the story, to piece together the real moments of it. Like anyone who was finally starting to figure things out would.

I called into work on Wednesday to get an extra day at my thinking. When I got my boss on the horn, he just laughed at me, told me not to bother coming back in at all, told me I'd already missed two weeks worth of hours and he was surprised I was even calling.

Delandra told me the Baron had found a red wig in Elizabeth's closet when he broke into her estate after she didn't return any of his phone calls. He was heartbroken, she said, and I could see him on the screen clutching the hairpiece in one hand and the bloody candlestick in the other, but he seemed more grief-stricken for himself than for either of the women he'd bludgeoned. He didn't seem to care about the time Elissa lost in her coma, or the moments Elizabeth was forced to lose. His only remorse was selfish. He pitied the freeze on his relationship. He thought his own story was frozen in waiting. Like me, like all of us here. Losing time to the will o' the wisp.

I told Delandra the Baron should learn to look around; that the real story was still going on; that he had it right because he'd learned how to break through the stasis. That he was still living within it. That I wished I could be that lucky. And Delandra stuffed flavored potato chips into her mouth and nodded as she stared at the screen.

I wanted to be like the Baron. I wanted to break through the wisp. I was losing more and more time everyday, more and more of my life. There were months gone. Passed due notices on rent tacked to my door. Repo men hauling off my truck. It was like I'd succumbed to a coma and the whole swamp was trying to swallow me up. I knew that if I could be like the Baron, if I could find a way to break through, that I would see the wholeness of my life. That I could feel the joys and the sorrows and not waste them in self-pity.

I started trying to focus on the details. I thought that if I could hone in on the minutia, I could ride out the wisp, each time widening my awareness until it lost its control over me. For weeks I sat atop Delandra's washing machine, searching for anything to ground me: the chip in the cinderblock step the caved into the dandelion strewn back lawn, the septic tank and its dull grey sheen that rusted out into an orange brown at the top dome, the battle of good and evil raging within Elizabeth/Elissa's subconscious mind. Nothing seemed to work. Time was escaping me, or I was. I thought of the Baron, of how he broke through.

Delandra's back door was unlocked, and I set the dryer on high with a pair of steel-toed work boots inside. The leather-covered metal rapped and clanged as the ricocheted around the hopper like every child in the neighborhood had taken to battling quartz with his aluminum little league baseball bats. I didn't have a candlestick, but I did own a crowbar. And like anyone would, I just wanted to feel something. I just wanted to be free. I just wanted to witness my own story. And the will o' the wisp had its way with me again.

There are partial truths that remain, exposed there in the ether like the branches of a winter oak, dripping with Demeter's tears over the loss of what she bore. Exposed and bone white and stained black with blood and matted hair. It don't snow around here much though. There's years in between the flurries. So we don't have much use for those pagan deities outside of the ones who keep the foxfires burning. Like anyone would, we pick and choose the parts we need, all what can make sense for the story. And the other parts, we dispose of. We keep the washer and the dryer and the snack cakes, and we let the swamp take care of the rest.

But it's in those parts when everything freezes momentarily, I guess it's those goddess tears up north and the brilliant wisp's will down here, that the story actually happens. Those are the moments of the divine that make it all come together and be linear and cohesive. Those are the parts we always have to make up. Those are the times that keep us free.

We Tremble As We Sink

THE POINT IS THAT WE'RE ALWAYS TRYING TO TAME SOMETHING, TO STAVE OFF NATURE, TO CULTIVATE OURSELVES, BUT IN THE END, THE WILD ALWAYS FINDS ITS WAY BACK IN

WE TREMBLE AS WE SINK

MAYMAW

Maymaw, when she got to be Maymaw around the time my older brother was born, took to traipsing about her yard with a sharp set of pruning shears, snipping away at the honeysuckle and the Cherokee Rose blossoms that grew wild along the side of her green-shingled house; cultivating them. That was Leroy's word. Cultivate. Leroy had studied horticulture at Alabama State before he'd come by this way to look at what he called the "prehistoric melding pot of the swamp" and before he'd met my momma and before he'd become my stepdad–but probably not before he became an ass-muncher–so he used words like "cultivate" where the rest of us all just said "tame" or "pinch back" or "rip off the fucking heads so's they don't rot the wood siding." We'd rather treat the cause than the symptom. Preventative medicine, Momma called it, even though it weren't so much preventing as masking. But that's why until I was ten I got a nightly dose of liver and castor oil. We tried to tame our bodies the same way Maymaw tried to tame those damn wild vines.

We lived a little ways north of her, but summer days I could cut through the backyards, kicking up the dandelion heads and sending Mrs. Bryar's hounds into a rage as I bee-lined through her yard. Momma would send me off with those huge skeins of acrylic yarn she'd pick up at the Wal-Mart, and Maymaw would use them to crochet those zigzagging afghans after her eyes got too blurry and her fingers got too frail for the quilting. Maymaw'd fix me up a PB and banana sandwich and get out her hook and tune the television to her stories, and I'd go out in the yard and search out the quartz arrowheads stuck there between the muddling of white sand and red clay.

Leroy'd always come looking for me just before sundown, saying that Momma had sent him to get me in before dark. But I knew it was just him trying to exert his newfound ownership over me by making me comply to his Rules for How a Proper Household is Run, or else hoping for a glimpse of Sue Ellen out watering her garden in the last glints of the sun's rays through the Cypress. Leroy'd been the one to tell her it was best to water her plants either early on in the morning or at dusk so the moisture wouldn't evaporate right out of the soil, so when he caught sight of her following his directive he got a double boner over her doing what he said and her in her tank top with the little spray of droplets that backwashed up from her hose glistening on her tanned skin. For her part though, Sue Ellen went with hosing down her plants in the evenings even though she was born here and raised here and anyone who was worth their salt 'round these parts knew that the pre-dawn moments were key so the excess water had time to evaporate during the sundrenched day hours and root-rot wouldn't get the chance to set in because she knew Leroy'd more than likely pop by in the evening time, and she liked the attention.

A few months or so back I'd wandered back inside to wash the dirt out of the crevices on the two arrowheads I'd dug out when Leroy showed up, so he took the opportunity to push around through the bushes and vines that separated Maymaw's yard from Sue Ellen's, angling to get a better view of Sue Ellen's tatas. Maymaw's stories were long over and the six o'clock newscast had just ended, so she'd grabbed her shears and gone out to do her business, snipping blindly at the hazy shades of green and tan and grey that encircled her yard. She'd nearly taken out Leroy's pinky, he'd been so wrapped up in the girl next door and had barely even noticed her approaching out of his periphery and pulled his hand away, yelping in an awkward and knee-slappingly funny way, and liked to give Maymaw a heart attack or triggered in her another stroke like the one that'd blurred up her vision. After that, Leroy was a lot more cautious when traipsing about the bushes, but it never really did stop him from doing it. Not until later.

During our Georgia history lesson for Social Studies, the teacher Mr. Cantrell let us each do a presentation for extra credit, and seeing as how I'd bombed the bit on the Bill of Rights earlier in the school year, I brought in my collection of arrowheads to show the class and figured I'd talk a little bit about the Indians who used to live in the swamp before we got here and took the land from them, making them walk away from their homes, eyes full of tears until they saw the casinos we were giving them and realized how much money they'd be raking in. Mr. Cantrell told me I should call them "Native Americans" and not "Indians," and Jessie Richards who'd gone up to Toronto with his family that last summer and thought he was cultured now in a way the rest of us backwoods, bog-born folk weren't insisted that even "Native American" was derogatory and informed us all instead that "First Nations People" would be the more appropriate terminology. Whatever. We got the land in the end, and we made it livable. They left behind their arrowheads and black hair and about one sixteenth of everybody's blood in the county, but they didn't leave behind any My Name Is... stickers so, I said, all of us could call them whatever we reckoned fit the best. Besides, way I saw it, "Indian" was the shortest and using that term gave me more time for the crux of my presentation: the seven fully-intact and eight more partial arrowheads I'd dug up myself from the yards around the town.

Lance Smithson cried foul and tried to get me in trouble. He'd almost gotten expelled from school once for bringing in one of his daddy's Playboys and neither me nor Jimmy Dicks—poor kid, but the ribbing had died down mostly by the eighth grade—had come clean about looking at it with him so Lance was looking for a means to get back at us and figured me bringing a set of weapons to school was a good enough way. The assistant principal had just laughed it off, guffawing over the notion that rocks would ever be considered as weapons in our civilized day and age, but said that for legal reasons due to the complaint he still had to call my parents in and send me home for the day. Things always get messy when legal reasons or permanent records get involved. Neither can ever account for the full story. Momma couldn't get out of her shift at the grocery store—they'd made her assistant manager in charge of produce—so Leroy was the one who showed up to collect me.

I saddled up into his pick-up, my quartz weapons at rest in a box on my lap. Leroy told me again about telling me I was wasting my time with digging up those old things and that I ought to be paying more attention to the living matter all around us. For instance, he was droning on, did I know that the whole swamp was only a couple of thousand years old? Older than Jesus, true, but not nearly ancient by the standards of the world–depending on whose clock you go by at any rate–and that the fascinating thing about that pre-historic melding pot was that, genetically speaking, it was like the inhabitants, plant and animal alike, had somehow reverted to their most base and wildest form. That somehow they'd overcome the taming of time and sprung up and out and majestic. He always did sound like a chode when he went on about natural processes. We stopped for lunch at the DQ, and he gave me the option of either going back out to the Park with him to help him finish cataloguing some samples or spending the afternoon at Maymaw's 'til he could swing by and pick me up.

I told Maymaw it was just me as the screen door bounced hard on the frame behind me. Following the sound of her stories com-ing loudly from the television, I found her spread-eagle on the arm-chair she had in the living room, a mostly drained bottle of bourbon or scotch or some other caramely liquor knocked over by her feet. Maymaw didn't drink, except for when she was thinking about Paw-paw, so I was beginning to rethink my decision to come here instead of the swamp. All of the sudden Maymaw's eyes popped open and she looked at me in terror, saying "Mitchell! What in the sam hell are you doing here? Danny's gonna be home any minute!"

Momma had tried to convince us that Mitchell, whose name showed up right after Maymaw suffered her stroke, was some char-acter from one of the soap operas who got soiled up in her brain with her real memories, but I was convinced that Maymaw'd had some torrid affair back when she was younger, especially since she was always worried about Danny–which was my name and I'd been named for my grandpa–showing back up to scold her tarty ways or join in or whatever it was that women past menopause thought about when sex was still trying to fight its way into the brain and the loins, like Leroy's swamp attempting to regain its territory. Like those vines that keep on coming back, or those "wild oats" that men are always trying to sow.

I poured her up a cup of water from the tap and set it up on the lamp table next to her for when she woke up again. I put the cork back in the bottle and put the bottle on the kitchen counter, then went back and covered up her body with one of her afghans, even though it was itchy, and awkwardly, for some strange reason or another, checked her pulse as I tucked the blanket around her neck. She'd been talking a few minutes before, but at her age, you just never know. She was still ticking so I left her be and sat down to watch some TV even though the networks don't make any advertising dollars off of kids stuck home from school so I knew there wouldn't be anything worthwhile bumbling through the airwaves.

I thought I heard the whine of Leroy's truck rounding the bend in the road about an hour later, but so many of the pick-ups around here had that mixture of gravel-dented mufflers and humidity-strained belts so it really could have been anybody. It woke Maymaw up though. She was mostly sobered, the slight slur in her speech more the product of her age and false teeth than the whiskey or the stroke. She mumbled something about her good-fer-nuthin' son-in-law and how he was always swinging 'round these parts but never visiting her. She asked me to check her mailbox for her and then went on talking to Mitchell who wasn't there so I put the cup of water in her hands and then slipped out to gather the junk mail. Momma'd had all her bills and official mailings rerouted to our place about a year and a half ago so as to make sure none of the important stuff got lost or misplaced. But Maymaw still liked to sort through the grocery store fliers and the Have-You-Seen-This-Child messages from the post office, imagining sometimes that she'd discovered a secret love letter that she had to keep hidden. Once I found at least twenty random post cards and Pennysavers stuffed under her armchair cushion. But it made her happy.

When I got out to her postbox, I caught glimpse of Leroy's truck parked a bit up the street, like he was trying to hide it behind the kudzu that had taken over a little ways down. He weren't inside the cab and he weren't at Maymaw's, so I started off toward where he'd parked to see if maybe he'd found some rare species of flower in the ditch or if he'd finally keeled over and we could all get back to normal. He wasn't there. I started back toward Maymaw's when I noticed that Sue Ellen hadn't closed up her blinds and was walking around with her milky breasts bouncing better than I'd even imagined the centerfold in Lance's magazine's breasts bouncing, and then they were suddenly cupped over and I'd recognize Leroy's stubby fingers anywhere.

I marched back over to Maymaw's and found her standing taut against her screen door, her eyes trained on the brush that separated her property from her neighbor's. She told me something to the effect of it looking like Mitchell'd done off and found him some new floozy. Then the rage melted out of her eyes and she offered to make me a PB and banana sandwich while I played in the yard.

I was out back still as the sun started setting and Sue Ellen came out her back door and started watering her garden down. I pretended not to be paying attention, and sure enough Leroy slipped out the front of her house and started to traipse his way over to fetch me. The lazy son of a bitch didn't even bother to bring his truck closer or walk up to the road so it'd be less obvious he'd been catting around. He gave a little wave to Sue Ellen and started making his way through the brush between the yards, his eyes trained so tight on the girl's body that he didn't even notice Maymaw out there taking her shears to all the vines and weeds like they were growing faster than she was able to snip.

Then came Leroy's scream. It was horrifying. Nothing like those yells and whimpers that were all throughout the horror flicks all my buddies and I watched together last Halloween. It was really gurgley and solid and real and falsetto. All of it at once. My flight instinct started to kick in, but I fought it and ran instead around the side of the house to find Maymaw's back to me and her shears bloody at her side and Leroy standing in front of her missing his thumb and crying. Not even looking for his thumb. Just standing there crying.

I like to think that Maymaw was trying to tell Leroy that he was an animal by removing his digit. That somehow she was commenting on opposable thumbs separating us from the wild and that Leroy had lost his 'cause he was no better than a hound out feeling for a bitch. I like to think that if it'd been out Maymaw'd have gone straight for his dick and snipped that out of the way too. That's how we were around here. Treating the cause and not the symptom. That's how we made things work.

Leroy and my momma divorced after that and he hightailed it back to Mobile or Huntsville or some other hick town in Alabama. They never did put his thumb back on for him because when the paramedics found it, it was too caked in dirt and had long since gone bad. Maymaw never got charged with assault or nothing because of her stroke and her drinking and how Leroy didn't want the news about him stooping Sue Ellen to get out so everyone just went along with it being an accident. He took the blame saying he shouldn't have tried to take a short cut on through the trees. He took the blame and then divorced Momma and then hightailed it out of town, looking for some other family who didn't mind a thumb-less jackass of a stepfather to try to "cultivate" them. I lost track of him after that. I had no desire to track him after that. But that's not really the point, where he ended up.

The point is that we're always trying to tame something, to stave off nature, to cultivate ourselves, but in the end, the wild always finds its way back in. We always succumb. Maymaw was probably one of the strongest women I ever knew, and no matter how many vines she clipped or papers she stashed or highballs she took, nature always worked its way back in. It seems only right then for us to stay here and watch them as they lower the coffin down. To not let them send us away like they like to do now; to make us eat sugar cookies and drink fruit punch in the church mess hall while they do the actual burying. We should, all of us, stand here and watch as they place her in the earth. That way we know when the seed was planted. That way we're all not surprised when the cycle starts on over and the wild starts trying to claim us all again.

Andrew Forrest Baker

WE
TREMBLE
AS WE
SINK

IT &
LAY
FALLOW

The land here is primeval. It's raw and untouched and every time someone tries to tame it, it figures out a means of reappropriation. It travels backwards in time. It's pre-Christian. Pre-man. It grows what it wants and washes out all of the shit and the sludge and the horrors that it don't need. It takes it all and it siphons it out and it longs for an innocence it can never hold.

And since we're here, since it can't seem to shake us off, it takes us in too. We become the guardians. We don't have to preserve nothing—it does that just fine on it's own. We just have to keep its secrets and from time to time expel its darkness.

We watch the clear waters turn grey and dismal without a single cloud in the sky. We listen as the creatures of the swamp go silent and retreat, and we fight the urge to cower. We tell the stories of the Pig Man and the Bog Witch and the lost souls, and the whole time we know that the swamp is dissecting our words, disintegrating them, picking them apart at the vowels. We know that the entire time the swamp is regressing forward to a place where even language can't touch it. Where the only stories told are in the haloed ripples left behind when the fowl dives down toward the frog.

A graduate of the School of the Art Institute of Chicago, Andrew Forrest Baker has published one novel and a collection of short stories. We Tremble As We Sink marks his second collection of stories, and a return to his southern roots in his writing.

His work has appeared literary collectives as well as hand-made 'zines that have popped up around Chicago. "'Cross the Line" previously appeared in Loose Change magazine.

WE
TREMBLE

AS WE

SINK

www.andrewforrestbaker.com

www.ingramcontent.com/pod-product-compliance
Lightning Source LLC
Chambersburg PA
CBHW020629250626
47154CB00004B/1743